Also by Gary Paulsen

ROAD TRIP

Jim and Gary Paulsen

WENDY
LAMB
BOOKS

Text copyright © 2013 by James Paulsen and Gary Paulsen
Jacket photographs copyright © by Eric Isselée/Shutterstock (top) and Erik Lam/ Shutterstock (bottom).

Visit us on the Web! randomhouse.com/kids
Educators and librarians, for a variety of teaching tools,
visit us at RHTeachersLibrarians.com

Library of Congress Cataloging-in-Publication Data
Paulsen, Jim.
  Road trip / by Jim and Gary Paulsen. – 1st ed.
      p. cm.
  Summary: A father and son embark on a road trip to a distant animal shelter to save a homeless border collie puppy.
ISBN 978-0-385-74191-0 (trade) – ISBN 978-0-375-99031-1 (lib. bdg.)
ISBN 978-0-375-98857-8 (ebook) – ISBN 978-0-307-93086-6 (pbk.)
[1. Fathers and sons–Fiction. 2. Automobile travel–Fiction. 3. Border collie–Fiction. 4. Dogs–Fiction. 5. Animal shelters–Fiction.]   I. Paulsen, Gary.   II. Title.
PZ7.P28432Ro 2013   [Fic]–dc23   2012014284

The text of this book is set in 12-point Berthold Baskerville.
Book design by Vikki Sheatsley

Printed in the United States of America
10 9 8 7 6 5 4 3 2 1
First Edition

This book is dedicated to
everyone who's ever
loved and been loved
by a really good dog
(and that includes you,
Debra Kass Orenstein).
And to all the dogs
who make us better people
by their example.
Woof.

Author's Note

Working on a book with my son never crossed my mind before this—Jim's a sculptor, not a writer, and I work alone—but he's got a great sense of humor and a way of looking at things I've always admired.

We talk on the phone nearly every day, and one day he mentioned having gotten a new dog. Like me, he collects strays and gets his dogs from the pound—we take the next one that's not going to make it and give it a home. We've done this forever; our family always has five or six dogs, all ages and sizes and breeds. I can't recall exactly what he said about how he came to discover that his new dog was in need of a home, but after I hung up the phone, I wrote a section about a father and a son rescuing a homeless dog.

I sent it to him even though I never send him books

I'm working on and the characters didn't have anything to do with us. A few days later, I got an email from him; he'd written a chapter about the characters on a school bus. I was surprised, but I liked what he'd done, so I added another section and sent it back to him. We never talked about what we were doing or had a conversation about how the story was unfolding. We just wrote and read what the other wrote and then wrote some more. And then our editor came in and tied it all together.

Maybe it's because we both love dogs that we could work together like this. I've written about dogs many times, and those books seem to have become my favorites. Even if it's not expressly stated or a part of the story line, I always think the characters in my books probably like dogs.

Jim and I lost track when we tried to count how many dogs we've owned over the years. But we've never lost sight of how much they added to our lives, and we can remember something about every dog we've ever known. We always encourage our dogs to expect that we'll share whatever we're eating with them, and we remembered the dogs who liked ice cream sandwiches and baby carrots and liverwurst. We can picture what each dog looked like sleeping and how some tucked into tight balls burying their noses under their tails while others slept on their backs, paws in the air, and still others slept with their legs out to the side like an *E* without the middle stick. We remember their games and their tricks and how, as a rule of thumb, dogs don't seem to enjoy practical jokes or being snuck up on. We recalled their births and deaths and how the world turns a different, brighter, softer color when a litter of puppies is born and then dims slightly when you have to say good-bye to an old friend.

Dogs never lie or cheat, and their default setting is love. Some may seem grumpy, but all dogs have honor, humor, and dignity, and if you're really lucky and you pay attention, they will bring out those same characteristics in you.

1

The Plan

"Are you sure this is a good idea?"

"Absolutely."

"Why?"

"Because I'm your father and I said so."

"That's really lame."

"But it works. We're going."

"That's what I thought." I lean against the pickup in our driveway and watch Dad shove the road atlas in the glove box without even looking at it.

Checking freeway numbers and plotting a route beforehand would be too traditional for him—he knows which direction he's heading and how to find the main freeway out of town; he'll figure out how he's getting where he's going when he's closer to getting there. That's how he rolls.

I don't roll like that, but I usually wind up going along for the ride. This time, literally.

Dad's always coming up with ideas for things for us to do together—rock climbing, sculpting class, fencing lessons, poetry slams, white-water river-rafting camping trips, helping the librarians organize a protest against censorship during National Library Month, ATV riding, and a photography class we took at the community center last year.

You'd think I'd be used to his spur-of-the-moment plans by now. But the clock on the dash says it's 5:17 a.m., and I didn't expect to be up this early on the first day of summer vacation. Dad shook me awake a few minutes ago and pulled me out to the driveway, talking nonstop: "We have to get on the road, now, right now, this very minute. Hurry up, Ben, we're burning daylight. We gotta hit the road."

I yawn, rub the sleep out of my eyes, and smile as I remember the rest of what Dad said. "There's a border collie pup who needs us. I just got an email from someone in the rescue group. We're going to bring him home."

We already have a border collie, Atticus, and we foster them sometimes when they're between homes, so I know how awesome they are. I love all dogs, even if they're ugly or yippy or they drool all the time or snort and wheeze. I even like the old, fat, waddly ones who can't control their pee. But border collies are extra special. They're not like dogs. They're more like control freaks with paws. They've been bred to herd sheep for generations, and even if they haven't been born and raised on a sheep farm, border collies are always trying to keep everyone in their world in check. Another border collie is definitely a good idea for someone like Dad. And maybe this one will like me best. Atticus has always preferred Dad, even though he tries to pretend not to. I can't really blame him; Atticus was part of the family before I was.

"Gimme fifteen minutes so I can get packed." I start back for the house.

"Packed? You're not making a grand tour of the capitals of Europe, you know. Couple days, there and back. I already threw skivvies and a toothbrush and a clean T-shirt and shorts in a paper bag for you. A sweatshirt, too. You're good to go."

I look at the crumpled bag he's tossed on the floor of the truck. I'm not at all sure that's everything I might need, even if it is just a two-day trip like he promises. I start a mental list: snacks, bottled water, a book, my iPod and the charger, my laptop, sunglasses, sunscreen . . .

Dad guesses what I'm thinking. "Travel light, Ben, so you can move fast."

He won't even let me brush my teeth or take a shower before we leave. I sleep in gym shorts and a T-shirt, so he considers me dressed. He does let me slip on a pair of flip-flops and grab my phone and charger from the kitchen counter.

He's revving the engine and has started edging away from the garage, so I hop in the truck and slam the door as he whips down the driveway in reverse. The house is a blur as we leave.

"How do you think Atticus is going to deal?" I tip my head toward our fifteen-year-old border collie sitting between us on the seat. He's staring holes through the windshield as if he's responsible for memorizing the route and is making note of landmarks and directions.

I'm not sure how Atticus will react to a new dog in the family, because I don't think he considers himself a dog. I get the feeling Atticus believes he's more of a person than a pet. He's old and kind of crabby. Plus, he ignores other dogs if they approach him. So I'm a little worried about how he's going to live with a new puppy.

Dad laughs. "Oh, he'll hate it. But they'll work it out."

That's his motto, I think: It'll work out. I pull out my phone and take a quick picture of Dad and Atticus in profile. Ever since our photography class, I take a lot of pictures and post them on my Facebook page.

"What did Mom say when you told her we were taking off?" Mom runs a tight ship and is very organized, but she's a lot more flexible than a border collie, so it makes sense that I'd have worried about Atticus's reaction before I thought about how Mom would take it.

"I'm going to stop by Colonel Munchies on the way out of town." He screeches around a corner and jerks the truck to a stop in the parking lot. He jumps out and says, "I'll just call your mother while I'm grabbing supplies."

Ah. He didn't tell Mom.

She probably wouldn't have been happy that we were taking a trip before we cleaned the gutters and painted the garage. So I'm pretty sure Dad's timed the call, hoping Mom will be in the shower before she goes to work so he can leave a message. But I bet she woke up and realized we were gone and she's been sitting at the kitchen table ever since, drumming her fingers and waiting for the phone to ring.

For a second I'm worried that Mom might put an end to our puppy rescue, or at least delay it until we get the stuff on her chore list checked off. But then I see Dad stagger out of the convenience store, loaded down with enough junk to keep us fed halfway across the continent, and he nearly drops the phone as he flashes me a thumbs-up. Nice. Dad's good at getting people to see things from his perspective. Plus, Mom loves dogs as much as Dad and I do, so getting her to say okay to the puppy was a no-brainer. Our sudden exit was the only wild card. Mom and I aren't as good with the unexpected as Dad would like us to be.

Atticus makes a noise like a snort. He's watching Dad on the phone. He cocks his head and flattens one of his ears, skeptical.

And Dad's not so good at getting border collies to see things from his perspective.

ATTICUS

I wasn't paying full attention when the boss and my boy were talking before we left. They were near the truck and the only thing on my mind was getting in the front seat before they left without me. They forget sometimes and try to drive off without me. When that happens, I sulk. Sometimes I chew a sock. Not a good one, but the next time, they think twice about forgetting me.

The boss is driving too fast. He always does when he's excited. And my boy has no idea what's really going on. I do, though, and I'm worried.

Plus, I don't want a dog. Getting a dog is a terrible idea. Dogs are not my favorite thing. Dogs are messy and needy.

The boy should have a dog, I suppose, because boys like dogs. But dogs are a lot of work, and I just know this one will not understand the pecking order at home.

Maybe they'll forget about getting a dog. The boss does forget things. That's why I always have to remind him to take me in the truck.

The Sucker Punch

Dad hops in the driver's seat after stowing supplies in the backseat of the cab. Instead of roaring out of the parking lot to hit the highway, he turns to face me and clears his throat.

"Ben," he says in a voice I don't recognize and that makes me a little sick to my stomach. "I have something to tell you."

"Uh-huh." I nod, though I'm sure something really bad is about to be dumped on me. Good news never needs that serious tone.

"I quit my job yesterday."

It's funny how five little words can make you go numb all over. I hold my breath, waiting for him to continue. And, I hope, get to the good part.

"I can't continue existing as a soulless midlevel corporate drone." He talks like he thinks I'll understand.

"Well, no, I guess that's not right," I say cautiously.

"I was suffocating behind a desk." This is news to me, but I nod as if I get where he's going. "I needed to get out in the real world and start working with my hands."

"Uh-huh . . ."

"I've started my own business."

"You did?" I struggle to remember exactly what it is Dad does for a living; weird how you never really pay attention to the things that matter, isn't it? He's a vice president in charge of, um . . . something for an insurance company. Mutual Fidelity Unlimited. I know that much because of all the pens lying around our house with the company name on them.

"Yes. Flipping houses."

"Excuse me?" I look at the clock again: 5:47 a.m. This is a pretty big change to take in before six in the morning. Has so much news ever come my way in such a short amount of time? We're going on a road trip and getting a new dog; Dad quit his job and is starting a new business called flipping. I'm a little dizzy and glad I'm sitting down.

"Buy low, renovate, sell high. It's a no-brainer."

"Oh." I think. "You're going to remodel houses? Like that show on TV?" That's scary. Dad can fix or build anything, but he's not great at finishing. I flash on our garage, which is packed with half-completed projects. Mom and Dad have to park in the driveway.

"Not remodel. Renovate."

"What's the difference?"

"Civic responsibility and making the world a better place, one crummy neighborhood at a time. The plan is, I'll go into a run-down area and buy a house in rough shape. After I renovate, not only will I provide some family a top-of-the-line new home and make a profit, but I'll have raised the market value of the entire neighborhood at the same time."

"What do you mean, 'crummy neighborhood'?"

"I bought our first place over on Fifteenth and Humboldt."

"You bought a crack house." I know that intersection from the news: a police car crashed through a wall during a drug raid.

"*We* bought a crack house." Dad beams. "Duffy and Son, that's our company name. Nice, right? Oh, and for legal purposes, it's a former *alleged* crack house."

"Well, that makes all the difference," I say, rolling my eyes. And wait just a minute here: "You *already* bought it?"

"I had to move fast to get it."

"Yeah, I bet former *alleged* crack houses are very popular." Dad always thinks everything needs to happen fast.

"I was sure you'd be more excited about this. I was counting on your support."

Fat chance. "Does Mom know?"

"Of course."

"And?"

"She's not happy."

"Define 'not happy.'"

"Your mother's problem is that she's looking at this from the wrong angle, son."

"What's the angle she should be looking from?" I hope he tells me something amazing enough to make the rising panic go away.

"That this is the start of a brand-new chapter in our lives."

I feel worse. He's delusional.

"Good chapters hardly ever start with houses where drugs have been sold," I point out.

"That's what makes this so cool—it's completely unexpected."

"We can finally agree on something."

"The future is ours, Ben. There's no limit to what we can do with this opportunity."

"Where'd you get the money?" The other day Mom said we couldn't stretch the budget to afford the new laptop I want. Lately we're eating more leftovers and she runs around turning off lights in empty rooms. She's been trying to talk to Dad about the bills over dinner, but he puts her off. They don't think I notice that he's been sleeping in the guest room lately.

Dad's phone rings. He looks down and tilts it toward me so I can see Mom's picture and phone number on his screen. The second he hits the answer button, I hear her: ". . . getting ahead of yourself . . . wish you had told me first . . ."

Dad shrugs and starts to get out of the truck to take the call. Before he shuts the door, I hear him tell her, "We'll work it out."

I wonder if Mom's stomach is as jumpy and tight as mine.

Okay, I never gave much thought to what Dad did for a living or whether it made him happy. Still, the fact that he quit his job and bought a crack house to fix up is a little terrifying. And kind of selfish.

I watch him pacing in the Colonel Munchies parking lot, phone to his ear. He's doing a whole lot of listening. When he catches my eye, he makes his right hand into a beak and taps his fingers and thumb together so I understand: Mom is talking his ear off. He gestures at me to take the phone. I shake my head; no way am I getting in the middle. Even though I'm curious to hear what she has to say.

I grab a half-empty bag of red licorice from the dash, and Atticus and I share breakfast while we wait for our folks to figure this one out.

I adjust the radio to a news station. We listen to inter-national events: same old, same old—economic sanctions, military invasions, overthrown governments. "By comparison, our day is relatively peaceful. It's all a matter of perspective," I explain to Atticus. He yawns and looks unimpressed by my wisdom. "Yeah, you're right," I admit. "When you have to compare your day to wars and market collapses in order to find the upside, you aren't in good shape." We each chew another piece of licorice and watch Dad head back to the truck.

He climbs into the cab, a big phony grin pasted on. "She thinks a road trip is a great idea."

Sure, she does: Mom likes her space when she's mad, and I bet she's mad enough to hope Dad stays on the road all summer.

I'm a little surprised she didn't insist he bring me back home. Even for Dad, this business idea and sudden trip is off the rails.

"Uh, one more thing," Dad says in the voice that makes my stomach do that alley-oop thing. I wish I hadn't just snarfed all that licorice. I might spew it all over the inside of the windshield. Depending on what he says. "We're going to have to live close to the bone for a while. Until the profits start flowing in."

"And . . . ?" This affects me how? is what I'm thinking, but that's too selfish to say.

"We might have to cancel hockey camp next month."

He did *not* just say that.

We've been talking about hockey camp since I was

five years old and got my first pair of skates. I'm finally good enough to hold my own with the other players on the A squad, and I pulled straight As all year. That was the deal: when I turn fourteen, if I get the grades, then I can go to hockey camp for six weeks.

"I know you're bummed, and it kills me to even think I might have to let you down, but for the time being, even with your mom working and me putting everything I've got into the new business to make it a success, there's a possibility I might not have the cash in time to send you."

"Mom would never let me down like this. What did she say about hockey camp?"

"She agrees that we can't afford it right now."

"So neither of you care that I killed myself to get those grades. For nothing."

No wonder Mom didn't make me come back home. She didn't want to face me after breaking her promise.

"You have to look at the bright side: there's still a chance everything will work out."

"How big a chance?"

He ignores my question. "And it's definite that you can go next summer. You'll be able to go *every* summer once the business starts turning the kind of profit I know it will."

"Our deal was *this* summer." Even I can hear how whiny I sound. Too bad; he deserves it.

"You'll work with me. It'll be great. No one else you know is going into business renovating houses with their dad."

"I don't build houses. I play hockey."

"That's why we're going on this trip—to spend some quality time together, talk about the business, and get you the dog."

"You think a dog is going to make up for missing hockey camp?"

"A dog makes up for everything."

"Not even close." I feel disloyal to Atticus saying that, but I've never felt so . . . resentful.

Atticus, who's sitting between Dad and me, is looking back and forth as we speak. He can tell something bad is happening—his ears are back and he's panting a little.

Dad's still talking but I've stopped listening, I'm so mad. The ice is the only place I feel comfortable, and my teammates are the best friends I have. They're all going to camp. The summer is going to be miserable and lonesome. Nothing to do, no one to hang out with.

Dad's voice changes and I start listening again. "I hate to say it, Ben, but I'm a little disappointed in your attitude."

"*You're* disappointed?" That's rich. My parents double-cross me and he criticizes me for being bitter.

Before I can ask him how I'm supposed to tell my

team that I'm not going to camp with them like I said, Mom calls. Again. This time he waits until he gets out of the truck and shuts the door before he answers.

This trip stinks like rotten eggs and untreated sewage and little green olives with the red things stuffed inside. The last thing I want to do is be stuck in a pickup with my dad for two days. But watching him talk to Mom on the phone, I realize I'd be more miserable at home with her, because she's mad at Dad and worried about money and would make me paint the garage.

At least I'll get my own border collie if I go with Dad. I've been wanting that—a dog that belongs just to me—for a long time. I have a list of possible names: Zamboni, Puck, Carom, Stanley . . .

And nothing says I have to talk to him or listen to him tell me about the business. I'll go, but I won't like it. No reason to be on my best behavior if hockey camp is out of the picture. And no matter how many maybes or mights he throws in, my gut tells me I'm not going.

I glance out the window and snap a picture of Dad talking on the phone—I might as well photograph all the elements of this trip—when I see the clerk from the store come out to grab a smoke. He looks kind of rough around the edges, like Theo.

Theo.

Perfect.

ATTICUS

I'm glad the boss and my boy were talking. But I don't think my boy wants to talk to the boss anymore. Then it will be too quiet in the truck and the boss will play outlaw country music on the radio loud and my ears will hurt. It's better when they talk.

Talking is always a good thing.

Even the new house is a good thing.

I saw the house the boss bought. And I saw the way his eyes smiled and his shoulders lifted when he walked through it. I don't know why he didn't try harder to tell my boy that he bought the house three months ago. Or that he worked on it at night and on the weekends and it's for sale and there's an offer already. The boss can't stand sitting around waiting to see if it works out, and that's why we're going on a trip.

The boy didn't notice that the boss was always gone and always tired.

I noticed.

3

The Criminal Element

Theo's a guy I know from school. He should have graduated this year, but he's missing a few credits. Our guidance counselors hooked us up because I'm a volunteer tutor and Theo needed someone to help him stay focused. I don't actually tutor him, since he's a few years ahead of me. We just get together to study. It must be working, because he'll graduate next semester.

When I first met him, he scared the crap out of me—he's got a shaved head and an eyebrow piercing. I'd heard about him around school. They weren't the kind of stories that scream future study buddy.

Getting to know Theo is one of the coolest things that ever happened to me.

I do all right for myself, friend-wise, but no one's knocking people down to hang out with me. Or they

19

weren't until word got out that Theo and I were tight. My stock rose after his street cred rubbed off on me. That's what I like to think. I noticed a lot more people sitting at my lunch table after everyone heard I was friends with Theo, and the guys on my hockey team keep asking if Theo's going to come to a game. This is what friends of rock stars and professional athletes must feel like.

Plus, Theo's just cool. No one else I know can talk about the subtext and dramatic irony of the play he's reading *and* the community standards for curfew violations and truancy. He's been in some trouble, but he's a good guy. Atticus loved him right off the bat.

Dad got a bad first impression of Theo when he overheard me telling my friend Todd that Theo had told me one of his buddies had been picked up for vandalism. Dad thought I was talking about Theo. He calls Theo "the hoodlum." I never bothered to correct him, because I liked the idea that Dad thought I was hanging out with a juvenile delinquent. Besides, Dad hasn't been around much lately.

Theo is exactly what this trip needs.

I dial his number. Theo picks up on the fifth ring, drops the phone, swears a blue streak, and says, "Five-fifty-six. In. The. Morning. This better be good."

"Sorry about the time. It's Ben. Got two words for you: Road. Trip." As part of his "I'm really serious about graduating" plan, Theo has been doing nothing but studying for months, and he's itching to taste freedom now that summer vacation has started. He lives with his older brother. I don't know where his parents are, so it's not like his folks are going to say no. Theo says his brother's only rule is "Don't smoke in the house."

"When do we leave?"

"We're on our way. Swing by your place in five."

"Good to go, dude."

I love Theo. I really do.

Dad does not. Which is what makes Theo essential for the trip.

The second Dad opens the truck door, I blurt out, "Theo's coming with us."

Dad doesn't say a word, just rests his forehead on the steering wheel. Welcome to my world, Dad. Now we're both miserable.

"How about a different friend? What about Todd? Let's bring Todd. Todd doesn't have a record and I've never seen his butt crack because his pants hang down too low, and Todd doesn't scare old ladies and little girls at the mall. Let's give Todd a call and drop the Theo idea. Whaddaya say?"

"Nope. Theo."

"Is it even legal for him to leave town? Won't his electronic ankle bracelet go off and alert the cops, put him in violation of some court-ordered restriction?"

"You exaggerate. Theo might seem rough, but he doesn't have an ankle bracelet and he's expecting us. We should get going." I point to the clock. "Weren't you the one in the big hurry?"

I can tell Dad wants to argue, but he's dying to get on the road.

"Fine." He slams the truck into gear, zips onto the road, and floors it. "But I am not—repeat *not*—posting bail for that kid if he robs a convenience store or mugs a senior citizen along the way."

"Understood. I don't think theft is his thing anyway." Dad flinches. I smile. "Take a right here. Third apartment building on the left."

Theo's standing on the street corner, smoking. He flips the butt away as Dad pulls up next to him, and climbs into the cab. Even though it's a big interior and Theo's in the backseat, his nicotine fug is gagging. Atticus wrinkles his nose and sneezes. Theo's taking off his jacket. He's wearing a sleeveless T-shirt. Excellent. No way Dad'll miss the homemade tat on Theo's arm. I turn to snap his picture and Theo flexes his bicep so that the tattoo really pops.

"Ben." Theo pounds my back as we pull away from the curb. "Ben's dad—how's it hangin'?" Awesome. Disrespectful to Dad and a bad influence on me in five words.

"You can call me Mr. Duffy." Dad's gripping the steering wheel so tight his knuckles are white. This might not be a totally horrible trip after all. I open a bag of barbecue chips and settle in.

"Can I smoke?" Theo asks.

"No," Dad says. "Not in the truck, not on the trip, not in front of my son."

"Got it. You one of those health nuts?"

"Just opposed to carcinogens."

"Sure." Theo shrugs and I'm a little disappointed he doesn't put up more of a struggle.

I hand Theo the bag of chips to take his mind off the nicotine fit he might be having and he starts crunching away. I pass back a can of soda, hoping he's the kind of guy who does big burps. That'll slay Dad. But Theo isn't a belcher.

"So, Theo," Dad says suddenly and in such a relaxed and friendly tone that I glance over in surprise. He winks at me, his Mr. Insurance Salesman, I'm-your-best-buddy wink. I bet he learned it at a convention. It means he's trying to work the situation to his advantage. He's probably hoping he can charm a confession out of Theo that will justify dumping him on the side of the road. I hope Theo hasn't got that kind of confession in him. I'm not sure how much of a past he's jammed into eighteen years. He doesn't like to talk about himself. "Tell me about school. Ben says you're really pulling your grades up."

That's an exaggeration. Theo passed all his spring

courses, but his GPA isn't anything to get excited about. And I've never talked to Dad about Theo's grades. I don't have a good feeling about this. Theo is supposed to make Dad's head explode trying to put up with him, not become his new best friend.

"Well, I don't know about that, but I stopped screwing around and got serious about school." Theo is obviously trying to impress. Dad nods, obviously impressed.

Man, *nothing* is going my way this morning.

"Impressive," Dad says. "What about after you graduate?"

"I'm planning to go to a community college to take care of my prereqs and get some decent grades. Then I'll be able to apply to the university." Dad's nodding like crazy, which is all the encouragement Theo needs to continue: "My guidance counselor said that with a GPA and a history like mine, that's the best plan. If I had known I was going to have to bust my butt this hard, I'd have taken high school more seriously, not skipped so many classes and so much homework, not to mention all the other stuff I pulled."

I knew Theo probably wasn't the kind of person who'd wind up in the middle of a street fight or the back of a cop car like Dad thinks. But I had no idea he could charm a parent this way.

My phone buzzes. Mom. I let her go to voice mail

and then text her the picture of Theo's tattoo with the message "We're bringing my friend Theo." Mom's not as freaked as Dad about Theo, but he's not her favorite person.

"Got a job lined up?" Dad and Theo are still mapping out Theo's future.

"Not yet, but I'll have to find work because there aren't any scholarships for a guy with grades like mine."

"I'm glad you came with," Dad tells Theo, grinning at me with an evil look in his eye. "Ben wanted to ask Todd, but I encouraged him to invite you instead."

Atticus barks. Sounds like "Liar" to me.

"So, what's the story with this trip?" Theo asks.

"Going to rescue a dog," Dad answers.

"Cool. I like dogs. Why take a road trip to get a dog, though? Can't you pick one up around here?"

"This one needs us." Dad hands Theo his phone. "Read the email I got. Read it out loud. So Ben can hear it."

" 'This six-month-old border collie was found on the side of the freeway, skinny and dehydrated, his paw pads scraped and raw from the asphalt. Due to overcrowding, it's urgent we find a home for him as soon as possible.' Wow. Rough start for the little guy."

"You can say that again," Dad says. "I had border collies when I was growing up. One saved my life, pulled me out of the street, kept me from getting hit by a car when I was a kid. Promised myself I'd never be without a border collie."

"Oh, hey, a picture." Theo holds it up for me to see.

Border collies, I swear, can smile, and this one has a big dopey grin that breaks me right down the middle. Especially to think that such a sweet pup had been dumped and left to fend for himself.

Theo's still reading: "'Approximately four million dogs and cats are put down each year because of over-population.' Man, I had no idea. . . ."

I swipe at my burning eyes and glare at Dad. "I'm making this trip for the dog; spending time with you isn't going to fix anything between us."

"So noted."

"How long are we going to be gone and where are we headed?" Theo ignores the bad vibes between Dad and me. "I left a note for my brother that I was taking off with you guys; I should text him a few details."

"A couple days, there and back," Dad answers.

"Don't let him fool you. We'll be lucky to roll back into town by Labor Day," I snort.

"Ben thinks I'm too impulsive to be trusted on a road trip," Dad says.

"Well," I say, "maybe it wouldn't have been a bad thing if you'd prepared a little before taking off."

"How?"

"Get the truck serviced?"

"The truck runs fine. It's just a simple trip. It's almost boring."

I feel a shiver run down my back. Dad is lots of things, but he's never boring. I hope I'm wrong to be worried. There's nothing I can do about it anyway except buckle my seat belt and hope for the best. I sit back and throw an arm around Atticus. He looks out the window like he's the one driving.

"Yup." Dad takes a swig of water from the bottle in the cup holder. "Nothing but smooth sailing from here on in."

ATTICUS

I wonder what the cat is doing right now. If I'm not around, he sharpens his claws on the side of the couch. I'm the only one who gets upset. I'm not allowed to bite—the people yell if I so much as snap at the cat—but I bare my teeth and the cat knows I mean business. He's probably sleeping in the sink, which I never allow, or sitting on the kitchen table licking the butter, which they always forget to put back in the fridge after breakfast unless I sit by the table and bark to remind them.

A dog is going to be a lot of work for me.

Maybe we'll keep the smoky-smelling big boy Theo, instead, and forget all about the new dog. He's keeping the boss and my boy talking. And he reached up and scratched the itch for me when he saw that I couldn't quite reach the right spot behind my ear with my back paw. He's good people. I can tell.

My boy thinks Theo doesn't care that he's not getting along with the boss. He does, though. I felt him tense up when they were talking even though he pretended not to see what was going on. He knows. I know that he knows.

The Bus

"Yup. You done thrown a rod."

"That sounds bad."

"Well, it ain't good, mister. This here truck is in terrible shape."

I glance at Dad from the other side of the open hood. We're all staring down at the engine. We've barely left home and we're already standing in a garage with a busted truck, which makes me feel hopeful that the universe has stepped in and put an end to Ben's Quality Time with Dad.

"To call you three candybutts would be an insult to stupid folks," the mechanic says like we've gone and ruined *his* truck. "Dummies like you drive their trucks into the ground. Hopeless. I seen a lotta nimrods like you. Always come when it's too late and then whine and complain about how much it's gonna cost. If you'da took care a your vehicle, you wouldn't a wound up with your bottoms in a sling like this, but you can't tell anyone anything these days."

Theo and I exchange a look and then he slides between me and the mechanic. Does he think the guy is going to take a swing at me or Dad for not taking care of the truck and that he needs to protect me? He might have a sixth sense about upcoming fights. And he probably knows I'm not really good with, um, conflict. Unless it's on the ice. Then I'm fierce. Not so much without a stick and all that padding.

"You sure it's that serious?" Dad asks, not seeming to notice that the guy's called him an idiot ten different ways.

"Of course I'm sure. I've had my head inside engines since I was old enough to stand on a wooden crate and look under the hood, and I been running this here garage since dirt was a fresh idea. I know everything there is to know about engines and a few things ain't been invented yet. When I say you done thrown a rod, you can take it to the bank: you done thrown a rod."

"We were making such good time." Dad shakes his head.

"Yeah," I say in my most sarcastic voice. "Nearly twenty miles before the truck broke down."

The mechanic—the patch on his shirt reads *Gus*—glares at Dad. "You know you ain't gonna go no further than that twenny miles for a right long time, don'tcha?"

"I got the feeling we were in for a delay when the truck started sounding like someone was hitting an empty aluminum garbage can with a hammer."

"How long will it take to repair?" I hold my breath.

"It's not a repair. I gotta rebuild the whole engine."

This is just like what Dad said about his flipping business. No one can *fix* anything anymore; they're all about *completely redoing*.

Gus keeps talking: "This ain't no tune-up. I'm gonna hafta put in new crankshafts and rod bearings, maybe pistons. Lots of times the whole thing has to be rebored. We're talking new rings, at least. Gonna have to order the parts first, which might take as long as a few weeks. Can't keep everything I might ever need on hand, ya know."

"Weeks?" I try not to look as happy as I feel. We can have the dog shipped to us, since Dad and I won't be bonding on the road. And maybe I can go stay at Theo's or Todd's until Mom and Dad settle things. Or until school starts next fall. Whichever comes first.

"Sucky news. We're going to pick up a border collie and I was kind of looking forward to meeting the little dude," Theo tells Gus.

31

"One a them black an' white dogs that herd sheep?"

Theo nods and jerks his head toward Atticus in the cab, looking out the window, pretending we're not here.

"Is that dog ignoring us?" Gus looks surprised.

"Probably. He's annoyed. I don't think he was too happy with the noise the truck made," I answer.

Gus chuckles. "He's embarrassed by what a fool yer dad is with vehicles." He snorts. "Smart critter. Why'd ya want another one if ya already got that one?"

"We're on a border collie rescue list. When one's been abandoned or needs a home, there's a bunch of us on a national email list who'll take them in. Atticus, in the truck, was a rescue dog once."

Atticus, as if knowing we're talking about him, turns his head and pretends to notice the mechanic for the first time.

"That there dog is sizin' me up, ain't he?"

I nod.

"Looks like he's barin' his teeth, but I know what a smile looks like. I like to see a smile now and again. Even if it does come from a dog. Nice fella."

"Once you get to know him."

"What happens to those dogs if you rescue people don't step in?"

"At most places, dogs only have so long to find a home or they're put down."

"Don't like the sound a that. I never had a dog myself, but that's not right."

"Our family fosters border collies; we keep them for a while till they find homes. This one, though—we're keeping him. He's mine."

Gus nods and starts to say something, but he's cut off by an awful noise.

BEEP. BEEP. BEEP. BEEP. Beepbeepbeepbeepbeep. BEEEEEEEEEEP. Someone's punching a car horn. We jump in surprise. I look next to me: no Dad. He'd gone poking around Gus's lot while we were talking. He's nosy; I should have expected he'd wander off and explore. I sigh and follow Gus and Theo as they head around to the back of the garage. Atticus climbs out of the truck and ambles alongside me. His head is down; like me, he's not looking forward to seeing what Dad's gotten into.

Dad is sitting behind the wheel of an old school bus. He stops honking when he sees us and waves.

"Took that bus in trade a while back. Didn't know what I was gonna do with it besides start a mighty fine rust collection, but who can pass up havin' their own personal bus?" Gus tells Theo and me.

"Very cool." Theo and I speak at the same time.

"I made it hum like it was brand-new."

"Did you need to get a special driver's license?" Theo asks.

"Yeah, never drove it, though. Where'm I gonna drive a bus?"

"Too bad," Theo says. "I bet it's a sweet ride."

"Always meant to take it out, never got round to it."

Dad comes bouncing out of the bus, grinning from ear to ear.

"I get the feelin' I'm gonna hafta keep an eye on yer old man," Gus tells me. "Worse than a bull in a china shop. Not the kind of guy ya wanna trust with too much rope, because sooner than later you're gonna feel it tripping *you* up."

"Yeah, pretty much." How did he manage to understand so much about Dad so quick?

"I'm a good judge of people, if I do say so. Got to be when you work for yourself like I do here. Can't afford to misread a fella." Gus reminds me of Atticus.

Gus, Atticus, and I watch Dad and Theo walk around the bus, kicking tires like either of them knows anything about it.

"We'll take this as a loaner while you're fixing our truck," Dad calls.

"The heck you will. I'd never let a complete stranger who can't take care of his own vehicle borrow *my* bus."

"I've always wanted to drive a bus," Dad says. "Even got my license for it a few years back. This is way better than the pickup. It's a statement: we support education *and* border collie rescue. What's the gas mileage on a thing like this? It'll be mostly freeway driving, once we get out of here."

"Is he hard a hearin'?" Gus asks me. I shake my head. "No," he says loudly in Dad's direction.

"We can put a banner in the rear window: BORDER COLLIE OR BUST."

"*N* period *o* period. No."

"You can come with." That's my voice. Dad looks at me and beams. Even Theo smiles. Gus studies the ground. I'm the only one who seems surprised I spoke up. What was I thinking? This breakdown was my ticket home.

"No one can ever say I don't pull my weight," Gus says. "I work seven days a week. You don't work, you don't eat. Don't believe in namby-pamby stuff like trips. No." He shakes his head, but he's still looking down, thinking.

Atticus leans against his leg to be petted. Gus ruffles Atticus's ears and nods. Makes up his mind.

"All right. Someone's gotta be there to check the oil. Make sure you get to that dog in time. And I don't like the thought of you two boys in the care of a man who doesn't look after his vehicle. Lemme get my toolbox and lock up."

We introduce ourselves as we collect our stuff from the pickup and climb into the bus. Gus tosses Dad the key, but sits where he can keep an eye on him, toolbox on his lap. Theo and I flop down across the aisle from each other. Atticus stands in the door and stares at Gus.

"Yer dog's lookin' at me like I'm settin' in the spot got his name on it, but I ain't movin'," Gus tells me.

Atticus grunts, real put out, but he jumps onto the seat ahead of me. Dad turns the ignition, grinding the starter.

"Turn it. Let it go. What's so hard about that?" Gus growls at Dad.

Dad tries gently and the engine purrs.

"Touch a motor right, she sings for ya." Gus tips his head, listening.

Even Atticus seems to sigh and settle back.

Dad adjusts the mirrors and studies the dashboard. Slowly, he backs up a few feet. Getting the feel of the bus, carefully maneuvering it between the cars up on blocks and piles of old batteries and tires, backing up and easing forward a little at a time. He gets the bus pointed toward the street without driving over or crashing into anything.

"If I can fix anything, this fella can drive anything," Gus says. "He's got the touch."

Dad turns onto the street without running over the curb. Then he guns the engine and we're smoking down the road.

Gus throws back his head and laughs. "Well, all right, then."

Theo and I high-five.

We watch Dad weave through city streets and get on the highway. Atticus moves over to sit with Gus, and I take their picture. Atticus smiles. Gus doesn't. I take a photo of Theo, too, even though what I get is him flipping me the bird.

I take a self-portrait. No photo of Dad. I text the picture of Gus to Mom. "We made a new friend after the truck broke down." She'll go out of her mind trying to figure out who the stranger is and what happened to the pickup. Excellent.

Like clockwork, Dad's phone rings. *He* can explain Gus And The Bus to Mom. Dad's probably going to use up all his minutes this month before lunch.

"Want some popcorn?" I ask Gus, digging through a sack next to me. I've got the morning munchies.

"Cheese or caramel?"

"I've got both."

"Caramel."

"Snacks are important." I toss Theo a bag of mini-donuts.

"Amen." Gus rips into his popcorn.

"How'd you wind up owning a garage?"

"Only thing I'm good at."

"I'm not sure what I'll be good at."

"Well, you're what, fourteen?"

I nod.

"Sooner or later you'll know. Find yourself where you're supposed to be without noticin' ya got there."

Theo speaks up. "Man, I hope so. That sounds like a sweet deal."

"It ain't easy; gotta work for it. You a good worker?" Gus is giving Theo a hard stare.

"I am now. Wasn't always."

"You two brothers?" Gus asks.

"Friends," Theo answers. I wish a speech bubble were over his head so I could take a picture of his answer.

Gus bellows, "Yer fool pa is gonna run us off the road he doesn't stop yappin' on the phone and start watchin' the road."

Dad straightens out the bus and salutes Gus in the mirror.

"Where's yer ma and why ain't she here, too?" Gus asks me.

"Why?" I can't see myself saying "My father spent our savings on some house-flipping/get-rich-quick scheme and I'm not talking to him because he screwed me out of hockey camp and my mom is glad we're gone." Especially to a stranger who might think I'm a huge baby for whining.

"Last thing we need is a woman," Gus says. "This bus is gonna remain woman-free."

ATTICUS

I like the bus. The truck felt crowded with Theo; it's usually just the boss, the boy, and me. I like having my own seat and being able to walk up and down the aisle and go from side to side looking out the windows. It's important to be able to see everything all the time.

Maybe we'll forget about getting a dog and just keep picking up new people. That's a better idea.

The man who smells like grease acted like he didn't want to come along, but he did. He got on the bus quick. And he's looking at my boy and the boss and Theo out of the corners of his eyes when he thinks no one notices. And he smiles a little with his eyes. Not his mouth, but with his eyes, which is always real.

5

The Brawl

"I don't mean to complain," I say to Theo, low, "but it seems to me Gus spent a lot of time on the engine and not much on the shocks." We've been on the bus for twenty more miles.

Theo nods. "Yeah, everything inside of me is either sore or bounced to the wrong place. And we just got started."

"I don't like what I hear," Gus says, tipping his head just like Atticus when he's listening hard.

"Dad's singing, right?" I call to Gus.

"Our complaining?" Theo guesses.

Gus snaps at Dad, "Pull over. Need to see what's going on with that engine."

I haven't noticed anything. It would take something pretty extreme to catch my attention. The pickup sounded like nails in a blender; the bus just sounds like a dull roar to me. Normal.

Dad takes the first exit and pulls into a strip mall parking lot. Dad and Gus are poking around under the hood before Theo and I hit the ground. We're stiff from the bouncing, so we walk toward the stores, Atticus at our side. I'm trying not to think how long this trip will take if we only get twenty miles before we have to stop again.

We're passing a diner just as some guy is being kicked out. His arm is twisted behind his back as he's propelled out the door. Theo and I dodge as he sprawls across the sidewalk, and we look past him to the person who threw him. It's a girl. She's a big girl, but I'm still surprised it's not a man doing the heave-hoing. Her name tag says *Mia,* and for the second time this morning, I think how cool it is when people are labeled.

Atticus moves between us and the guy on the ground, and the hair on his neck goes up. He doesn't bark or even growl, but he drops his head and raises his butt and backs away from the guy, trying to edge us farther away from him by nudging us with his hip.

"Get your filthy mouth out of here, Bobby," Mia says in a calm voice. "I told you I wouldn't stand for that."

Bobby staggers to his feet, about to say something to her when he catches sight of Theo. Theo ducks his face and grabs my arm. Before Theo can drag me away,

Bobby takes a swing at him. Theo moves out of range and Bobby's punch misses him, but the momentum—and Atticus's nip on his ankle—knocks Bobby off balance and he teeters into Mia.

She slaps both hands on his shoulders and shoves him so hard I swear I see snot come out of his nose when he lands flat on his butt on the sidewalk. He makes a weird sound—I think she's knocked the wind out of him. His mouth is opening and shutting like he's a fish in an aquarium. Atticus makes a panting noise that sounds a little like a laugh: "Heh heh heh."

"I've had it with this place," Mia tells Theo and me. "This is the third loser I've had to toss this week and I am over it."

Bobby gets to his feet, glares at us, and snarls, "This ain't done." I think he's talking to Mia, but he seems to be looking at Theo. Weird. Bobby limps away and the three of us exhale. Mia glances from Bobby to Theo and lifts one eyebrow. Atticus sits down, the fur on his ruff still raised.

"You handled yourself like a pro," I tell Mia.

"Bouncing bad customers wasn't in the job description. I can't take this anymore. I'm quitting. Wait right here." She storms back into the diner. For some reason, Theo and I do as she says and stay put. I look at him and he shrugs. I pull out my phone and take a picture of Atticus in front of the diner. I wish I'd thought to take a picture of Bobby, but I'm not really an action-cam kind of guy. I point the camera at Theo.

His eyes are locked on his phone. He's having a text conversation with someone. His thumbs fly and he chews his lip while he waits for the reply. It's not warm, but he's started to sweat. I can see dark patches under his arms.

Mia comes flying out. "Okay, *that's* done. Oh my gosh!" She's looking at me. "You're bleeding!"

I am? I reach up to touch my face.

"There's blood! Did Bobby come back and hit you?"

"Oh, uh, no. Um, well, see, stress gives me nose-bleeds. Sometimes."

"He's barely bleeding; it's just a few drops." Theo studies my face. He thinks Mia's making a big deal over nothing. She puts her arm around my shoulder. I slip an arm around her waist, lean against her. Theo rolls his eyes. Probably wishing he were the one with the bloody nose. I smirk at him as Mia leads me to a bench.

"Here, tip your head back. I've got some tissue in my purse." Mia crams tissue up both my nostrils.

"Nice look." Now Theo's the one who smirks. "Let me take *your* picture."

I shake my head and snap a picture of the bloody tissue I pull out of my nose.

"Do you know Bobby?" Mia asks Theo. "Looked like he recognized you."

44

"He's someone I used to know, yeah. More like a non-friend of a friend."

"He didn't look friendly when he tried to deck you."

Theo's phone buzzes and he checks the text, frowns, and shoves the phone back in his pocket. He's gnawing on his lip.

"Were you guys heading into the diner?" Mia asks.

"No, just stretching our legs. Rest stop," I tell her.

"Road trip? Cool. Where you headed?"

"We're on a quest to save a life."

"Shut. The. Front. Door." Mia's mouth is hanging open.

"Yup. There's a dog who needs our help and we're going to save him from certain death." I sound just like Dad. Now I get why he's like that: I'd say anything to see that look on Mia's face.

"I love dogs." As if we couldn't tell—she's feeding Atticus a sandwich she pulled out of her bag and not even getting squeamish that he's drooling all over her foot. "I'm Mia, by the way."

"I'm Ben, this is Theo, and Atticus is the one slobbering on you."

"Are you brothers?"

"Friends," Theo and I answer together. Nice.

"That's my Dad and Gus." I point to them still working on the bus.

"You're going to rescue a dog in a school bus?"

"It's kind of a long story." It's not even lunchtime and my day is already a long story. Geez.

"Did you steal the bus?"

"Um, no, why would you ask?"

"*That* would be a long story," she says. "I stole an ATV once. And a small sailboat. And a snowplow."

"Did not."

"Well, not at the same time. But you can see why I asked if you stole the bus."

"Ohhhh-kaayyy." Is this what career thieves or compulsive liars look like? She's probably eighteen or nineteen, and there's a lot of her crammed into a little waitress uniform. I count six earrings in the ear facing me, and she's got purple and green streaks in her hair. Black fingernail polish and red cowboy boots and a ton of noisy bracelets. She's not pretty, but there's something about her that makes you keep looking, and the longer you look, the more interesting she is. I've never seen anyone like her.

Theo's checking her out, too. "Did you really just quit your job?"

"Yeah. I should have left months ago. It's a hostile work environment. Sharkey, he's the owner, said the uniforms brought in the big tips. He's the kind of perv who orders the uniforms one size smaller than what the girls tell him. The hem's always creeping up and there are buttons missing in the front so you're showing the goods more than you'd like. Still, he promised that they didn't allow touching, it's policy. So when Bobby patted my bottom and said 'You might as well go out with me because I'm gonna tell everybody we did anyway,' I'd had enough."

"What are you gonna do now?" What is with all the up-and-quitting jobs today?

"Follow my dream. This job just paid the bills while I got on my feet."

"What's your dream?"

"To be a triple threat."

The only triple threat I can think of is the football player who can run, pass, and kick. I don't think that's what she means, even though she's, um, hefty enough to hold her own on a football field.

Theo asks, "Singer, dancer, actor?"

"Not the kind in football," she laughs. I turn red, embarrassed that I thought that a minute ago.

"Are you any good?"

"So far I'm just good at being told 'You're not really what we're looking for' and 'Come back when you have more experience.' "

"Bummer."

"Your dad's waving at you. Introduce me." She's halfway across the parking lot before I can get to my feet. Theo and I jog after her.

"Hi, I'm Mia." She's shaking hands with Dad and

Gus. "These guys just gave me the guts I needed to make a major change."

"There's a lot of that going around." Dad smiles at Mia and raises his eyebrows at me. I look away; it's cute when *she* does it.

They're chatting about chasing dreams; I'm not really paying attention. I'm watching Atticus watch Theo texting. Atticus is sitting with one paw raised and he keeps reaching out to scratch at Theo's leg. He wants Theo to put the phone away. So do I.

"So, how about I come with?" Mia's asking Dad and my attention is back on their conversation. "I'd like to help rescue a dog."

"It ain't a real bus route, ya know, stoppin' to pick up people along the way," Gus grumbles from under the hood. She looks over his shoulder.

"Nice ride. In-line six-cylinder, four-stroke-cycle diesel engine, right?"

"Finally. Someone who knows engines." He glares at the rest of us. Mia's in and we all know it. She texts her roommates to let them know she's going on a quick trip and will be back in a couple of days.

She makes Dad show her his license and she sends his info along to them. She snaps a picture of all of us beside the bus and sends that, too, with our names. "No offense," she says. "But a girl can't be too careful these days." We all nod.

"How do you know about the engine?" I ask Mia.

"I know a little bit about a lot of things. You never know when you're going to need stuff, so I try to keep my eyes open."

"We're not sure how long we'll be gone," I try to warn her. "Dad's not really a planner." I hope he hears the disgust in my voice even as I hope Mia doesn't. I wish there was a way to be charming to her and make Dad know I'm mad at him. "We're supposed to be in a hurry to get there, but I wouldn't count on it."

She shrugs. "I can take a couple days. It'll be a good story. A person in my line of work needs to collect life experiences; makes my art more authentic."

"Saddle up, then. We're heading out. Put some ice on that nose," Dad says to me as he jumps on the bus, Gus, Theo, and Atticus behind him. Mia and I drop into seats as the bus lurches out of the parking lot. Theo hands me a wad of paper napkins filled with ice from the cooler.

I watch Atticus hop onto the seat and lean against Mia as he looks out the window. She puts her arm around him and nuzzles his ear. I take their picture. Mia grabs the phone, studies her image, and makes me take another one she likes better. "Always looking for good head shots," she tells me. "And a picture with a dog will make me more memorable. He's very handsome."

I take a couple of shots of my iced nose and send

them to Mom. She's sent a few texts. I press Save without reading them. Maybe later.

Theo's texting again, chewing on his thumbnail. Gus seems to have fallen asleep. Dad's singing along with the radio.

I take the ice away from my nose and check for a new leak. I'm good. So I've stopped dripping blood and I'm sitting on a school bus talking with a kinda-hot girl who's just decided to run away with us. I usually have trouble talking to girls. I'm pretty shy and can never think of what to say. Apparently rescuing a dog makes it easy to keep a conversation going. Good to know, though I'm not sure how many times I can use the technique. Probably more than the average person, given how nuts our family is about dogs and saving them from being put down.

"I like you, you're impulsive," Mia says.

I glare at the back of Dad's head. "It kind of runs in the family."

"You don't sound happy."

"Not so much." Because pretty soon I'll be quitting good jobs and disappointing kids. It's a slippery slope, this impulsive thing. And she should talk. She just walked away from her job and got on a bus with a bunch of strangers to rescue a dog.

"You guys have a beautiful aura," she tells me.

"That's not something a person hears every day. What's it mean?"

"You have good energy, I can tell. I'm sensitive to that, and chakras. It's a gift."

This is turning into a very weird trip. But a few hours ago, I thought I'd be stuck in the truck listening to Dad, and here we are on a bus with three other people and I'm eight rows away from him with a girl who's getting prettier all the time. And she's smiling. At me.

ATTICUS

The girl who smells like pancakes and bacon, Mia, points out the cows on the side of the road and then we bark at them. No one else thinks this is a good idea. They're wrong.

I'm going to have to bare my teeth at Theo and my boy if they look at her that way again. I lifted my lip at them when they hesitated by her seat the last time we stopped for gas, and they got the message and sat behind her. She's mine. They can talk with her, but they can't sit next to her.

I've seen the Bobby person who tried to hit Theo. My boy and I were taking a book to Theo's apartment and he was in a car parked at the curb. Waiting. And when Theo answered the door, his shoulders were tense and he kept looking past us. I think Bobby was right when he said it's not over. Theo knows that and that's why he keeps texting. Mia knows, too; that's why she keeps watching Theo.

6

The Fiery Inferno

"Does anyone but me care that we have no idea where we're going or how long it's going to take to get there?"

I get a chorus of sleepy no's. We've been on the road for six hours, one speeding ticket, four pit stops, and one drive-thru crisis (Dad wrongly guessed the height of the bus and we took out the lane sign at a hamburger place).

I know we only left home this morning and we're on a well-traveled interstate, but I have visions of running out of money and gas and being forced to live in the wilderness with Dad. He'll love it. He's probably hoping we'll have to eat small animals we catch with sticks, and strain drinking water through our underpants from puddles on the side of the road.

"I could listen to this engine purr for a long time,"

Gus says. He's sitting in the seat behind Dad, clutching a wrench and eyeing the gizmos on the dashboard, hoping, I guess, that something goes wrong under the hood.

"The further the better," Theo says. "And it's good to see some other sights." He tries not to, but throws a quick glance in Mia's direction. She notices and blushes. Atticus growls at Theo and I hide my smile.

"Dude, I think your dog is into Mia," Theo says under his breath.

"That makes three of us," I whisper back.

He laughs. "Yeah."

"I was born to travel," Mia says, breaking up our huddle, "like maybe I've got gypsy blood." She suggested road bingo, Twenty Questions, I Spy, the alphabet game, and Slug Bug, but no one took her up. She must be making a list of license plates, because she happily whispers "Nevada" or "Vermont" to herself and scribbles in her notebook. I take a picture of Atticus resting his head in her lap.

Dad says, "I've been itching to take a trip for a long time."

Who asked you to chip in, Mr. It'll All Work Out? Then it hits me: I've been with Dad for hours and we've barely talked. And my mother's been trying to reach me all day, but it's easy to avoid her. I could stay on the road forever. Or until my parents get their business straightened out. If they can't afford hockey camp, can they afford me anymore? Could I have myself declared emancipated? It's extreme, I know, but it'd be so cool living on my own. Maybe Theo and I could get a place and—

"STOP THE BUS!" Gus roars. The tires squeal and leave black smoking skid marks on the asphalt as Dad stamps on the brakes and the bus comes to a shuddering stop in the gravel on the shoulder of the road. Atticus is barking like a lunatic.

Dad leaps up and hurls himself down the stairs. I'm on my feet before I know what's going on, flying up the aisle, hot on Dad's heels, charging to the front door. When Dad and I clear the bus and land on the pavement, we look behind the bus. There's a burning car on the side of the road about twenty yards from where we've stopped.

The car has a few flames darting out from under the hood. Dad and I sprint to the car in what feels like less than a second. He won't let me close enough to see if anyone's inside—he's trying to stay between me and the car. We're squinting through the smoke from a few feet away, but we can't see inside. Dad takes another step toward the passenger door, shoving me farther behind him. I surge forward, shoulder to shoulder with Dad. Just then, the burning engine makes a freaky, deep *wa-hump* and the flames leap up. I hear Mia scream. Atticus barks and Gus shouts, "Get back!"

Dad leaps backwards, yanking me with him. He waves the smoke away from his eyes but keeps heading for the car.

"Wait! I'll be right back." I pull Dad away from the car and gesture toward the bus.

I remember having seen a fire extinguisher by the driver's seat, so I race back, catapult myself up the steps, wrench it free, and tear back. Dad's circling the car, trying to get closer. He's got an arm in front of his face, still trying to look inside the car. I push him out of the way, but my hands are shaking so hard I can't hold the nozzle. He takes the extinguisher from me and points it toward the engine while he squeezes the lever. A spray of white foam muffles the flames and the fire is out. Dad and I take a closer look inside. Empty. All that worry for an abandoned car.

We each take a deep breath. I don't know about him, but I'm shaking all over and my eyes are watering from the smoke. I look in the ditch at the side of the road: no one. Dad's scanning the road in both directions. Neither of us can see anyone who might have been driving the car.

All this time cars have been passing us by on the highway. Not a single person stopped to help, though plenty slowed down to look. It was just Dad and me.

We turn back toward the bus. Gus is bent over, catching his breath. From trying to run, I guess. He *is* pretty old. Mia's patting his back, trying to get him to take a sip of water, talking on her cell phone. Who's she calling—the fire department? The police? A news helicopter? They always seem to have footage like this on the evening news. Theo's eyeing the car and pacing the shoulder. He keeps glancing at his phone and staring into the trees near the side of the road. The wet patches under his arms are back even though it was Dad and me who ran to the car. Atticus is glued to Theo's side, his eyes locked on Theo.

"I can't believe that just happened," I tell Dad.

"And Gus said *I* was hard on my vehicle." Dad laughs.

It's the most we've spoken since this morning. Dad opens his mouth, but before he can speak I turn and walk to the bus. I'm not ready for a heart-to-heart yet, even though we did just save each other's butts. I'm too shaky. We walk in silence but I reach over and grab his arm when he stumbles a little. We pretend not to notice. Or that I'm leaning on him, too.

"You guys are so brave." Mia throws her arms around me and squishes me in a big hug. I'm having trouble breathing, but I don't try to pull away. "The rest of us didn't know what was going on. But you ran toward the fire without a second thought. Like you knew exactly what to do."

"It was boneheaded," Gus says, scratching his head,

"but you looked pretty fine doing it. Crazy." He pats Dad and me on our shoulders.

Theo doesn't say anything; his thumbs are flying over his phone. I hope he's telling all his friends what Dad and I just did. It'd be cool to have the word spread around town before we get home. He probably took pictures; I'll have to ask him to forward some to me later. Atticus whines a little as he leans against Theo's leg. Poor guy. I sit next to him on the shoulder of the road and wrap my arms around his neck. He licks my cheek and I feel the shaking start to fade. My hands feel steadier the longer I pet him.

A cop car, an ambulance, and a fire truck come screaming down the highway, followed by a tow truck. Mia must have called everyone. I take the pictures of the men as they climb out of their rigs. It must be boring for them—nothing but a smoking car, four shaky people standing around, and an anxious border collie. And Theo pacing back and forth, texting.

Dad walks over to the policeman, who jots notes as Dad gestures at the car. The paramedics start for us, but we wave them away with thumbs-up; no one's hurt here. They get back in the ambulance and take off. Once the firefighters see that the fire is out, they climb back onto their truck. The tow truck guy loads the ruined car onto his flatbed. I snap a picture, kicking myself that I didn't think to take out my phone when the engine was still on fire. That would have been the most dramatic picture I ever took. I'll have to ask Theo if he took pictures or just stood there texting.

"I never saw a car fire before," I say.

"As these things go," Mia says, "it was pretty tame. Sometimes the tires explode."

"Why do you know so much about burning cars?"

"I dated a guy who was kind of known for car fires."

"How does someone get known for *that*?"

"Insurance scam. Getting rid of evidence. Making a point about territory. You know—there are lots of reasons to set fire to a car. He knew most of them." Mia sounds almost . . . breezy.

"What kind of aura did *he* have?" I ask.

"Very dark and heavy."

I look over at Theo to see his reaction. Nothing. He's pacing and texting. Atticus is trotting back and forth next to Theo, his eyes never leaving the woods on the side of the road.

"What kind of riffraff have you gotten caught up with, missy?" Gus snaps. "Sounds like the kinda people who'll steal from ya, gut ya, leave ya for dead in the ditch." He notices Mia's expression. "Don't act so surprised. These things happen."

Before Mia can answer, Dad heads over to us as the cop drives away. "Back in the bus. We've got a border collie pup waiting for us."

We all climb on, and Dad pulls into traffic. Atticus must be rubbing off on Theo, because he keeps looking out the side windows and behind us. Atticus surprises me and sits not with Mia, but next to Theo. From my seat behind them, they look like their heads are connected, the way they swivel together looking out the windows. Theo pulls out his phone when he gets another text. It reminds me.

I send a text to my mom. I need a few screens to tell the whole story of Dad and me and the fire.

"Dad." He nearly drives off the road at the sound of my voice. Can't blame him after the silent treatment I've been giving him. "I just texted Mom, told her what happened."

"Thanks, son. I better call her, reassure her we're okay. Gotta call the girl who's holding the dog for us, too, let her know—"

"—that we're hopelessly lost but making good time." I finish his sentence. It's an inside joke from the Boy Scouts hiking trip we took a couple years ago.

It's good to see Dad smile at me in the rearview mirror. I smile back, but just a little one so he knows we haven't worked everything out yet.

ATTICUS

The car that was on fire was the same one I saw Bobby sitting in outside Theo's place.

As soon as he saw the car, Theo started looking along the side of the road. So did I. We didn't see anyone. Theo stopped looking once he started texting. I kept looking. I couldn't smell anything because of the smoke. I know Bobby's smell from when I bit him this morning.

When the cop came, Theo pulled up the hood on his sweatshirt and kept his face down.

Theo's ice cold when I lean against him, but he can't stop sweating.

When we got back on the bus, he jammed all his stuff in his bag that had been on the seat next to him, and he's holding the shoulder strap so tight his knuckles are white.

We're both watching out the windows. Because someone is after him.

7

The Drag Race

"Uh, Dad? How fast are you going? It feels like we're flying, and speeding in a bright yellow school bus isn't the kind of thing that slips under the radar."

Radar.

As soon as the word leaves my mouth, I know I've jinxed us. Sure enough, I hear the sirens and see the lights from behind. Dad mutters to himself and jerks the bus to the side of the road, spewing shoulder dust and pebbles in our wake.

"Another cop." Theo sighs and rubs his face.

"Another ticket." Dad sighs and rubs *his* face.

"Another delay." Mia bites her lip. "I know your dad says it'll all work out, but I'm worried about getting the dog in time."

She's not the only one. His picture flashes through

my mind and I get edgy. I hope Dad's been keeping in touch with the shelter to let them know we're on the way.

Gus turns in his seat to watch the cop walk to the bus from where he pulled in behind us. "Yup, we just blew past the duck pond. That's what they call the place off the highway right outside of town where cops sit an' wait fer fools to speed."

"Walked right into that one," Dad agrees.

We all stand and exit the bus together. The cop is the poster child for the police academy. Spic and span. I straighten up and square my shoulders as he approaches. Theo slumps against the side of the bus. Has he been wearing that baseball hat all day? I don't think so, but now the brim is pulled down so low I can't even catch his eye.

Mia smiles and waves, like this might be a social call. The cop raises a hand to wave back but then tries to act as if he's lifting his arm to gesture to Dad to move closer to him. Nice save.

Dad walks toward the cop and Atticus follows. I suddenly realize our dog is not on a leash, nor does he have a license or ID tag on his collar. My mouth is too dry to whistle Atticus back to me. I can only hope this guy has a soft spot for dogs and won't add an off-leash violation to our ticket.

And I know we're going to get a ticket by the way the

officer taps his citation book against his thigh. Dad's gotten a ton of speeding tickets. The last one was this morning. So I should be used to the routine by now. But there's something about a law officer walking toward us writing a ticket that puts fear into my gut.

"Good afternoon, Officer. How fast did you clock me?" Dad asks. I wish I didn't know that he wants to find out if he's broken his personal record.

The cop looks uncomfortable.

"I don't need independent confirmation to know that that bus was going well in excess of posted speed guidelines."

"Oh, well, then: How about you let me off with a warning? I'll drive more slowly, and we can all be on our way." Dad's negotiating. That's how he describes trying to hustle out of a ticket.

"Do you have a license to drive a bus, sir?"

"Yes, I do!" Dad pulls out his driver's license and hands it to the cop with a big grin. "And I'll save you looking it up on the computer: I already got a ticket for speeding today."

"Sir, this is not a joke. Keeping the roads safe is the duty of every driver and every police officer."

"Aren't you going a *little* overboard?" Dad asks.

"Uh . . . Dad?" Giving the cop a hard time? That's the *best* idea you have right now? My head's about to explode. I glance over at the cop and see the nameplate pinned next to his badge: *Sgt. Laurence.* I wish *everyone* wore a name tag; this is the third time today it's come in handy.

"Would it help if I told you I was speeding for a good reason? We're hurrying to save a dog—a homeless puppy, actually—and staying at the speed limit isn't getting us there as fast as we need to." Dad holds up his phone with a picture of the puppy. Sergeant Laurence waves it away. Not a dog person. Bummer.

"It's dangerous. There's a speed limit for a reason and that reason is public safety," the sergeant says, winding up to give a lecture.

"I'm a very safe driver," Dad says with a straight face. I could strangle Dad right now. Or turn and start walking home. Theo looks like he's considering it.

"My job is keeping the roads safe, one speeder at a time. And if I happen to write the most tickets in the entire department every month, well, so be it."

Oh, great: Dad and the cop are both competitive.

I catch sight of Gus walking around the cruiser, examining it. He pokes his head in the driver's seat window and studies the dashboard. Sergeant Laurence must see me looking past him, because he turns, does a perfect double take, and hurries toward Gus.

"You. Step away from the cruiser and produce your license." Dad, Atticus, Mia, and I follow him toward the cop car. Theo hangs back.

"Nicer'n I thought a cop's ride would be," Gus tells him. "Speedometer says this thing goes one sixty. You ever taken it that fast?"

"Got to ninety-eight once, in pursuit, but— Just a minute." He turns back to Dad. "We're talking about *your* speed limit."

"I've always wanted to get behind the wheel of a police car," Dad says. "Mind if I just slide in, see what it's like?"

"It's not an amusement park ride."

"Should be," Gus says.

The officer almost smiles.

"What's going on?" I whisper to Mia. Are we going to get the ticket or talk about cars?

"Guys and cars," she whispers back. "Shhh, don't ruin it. They're bonding."

"You ain't felt nothin' till you've driven a bus," Gus tells him. "Wanna try it?"

"How's it handle? But—wait—I'm giving him a ticket. We're not test-driving each other's cars."

"How about we race instead?" Dad says. "I lose, you write me the ticket. You lose, we shake hands and walk away with a warning."

"Uh, Dad? That's not—I mean, um, asking *a cop* if he wants to, uh, drag race? Really?" I step forward and give the cop a shaky smile. "I'm sorry, Sergeant, but my dad, um, well—"

"—has a great idea." Sergeant Laurence looks as shocked to have said those words as I am to hear them. "It's wrong, I know, and rules were not made to be broken. But . . . but . . ." He's trying to do the right thing, I can tell. "But I want to drive that bus and I've gotta see how fast my cruiser can go!"

"Let's roll." Dad opens the car door and slides behind the wheel.

I want to say "Dad! You're crazy!" and remind the cop this is not a safe-road kind of deal, but Mia is squeezing my arm, her eyes glowing. Atticus is shifting his weight back and forth; he's picked up on Dad's excitement. Even Theo is lurking behind Mia, peeking out from under his cap, waiting to see how this goes down. So I keep my mouth shut.

Sergeant Laurence reaches in the cruiser and disengages the camera, makes a quick radio call, telling someone named Marlene, "I'm taking a coffee break for the next ten minutes."

"It's not a race," he says to Dad. "Just let's see how long it takes both of us to accelerate from this spot to that billboard." He points to a sign a few hundred yards down the highway that's so deserted and straight it seems to have been built for a speed test.

"No big deal," Dad agrees.

I feel dizzy and look around. Not a car in sight. Sergeant Laurence, Dad, and Gus are all bouncing slightly, trying to contain their energy.

"You ain't never gonna believe how that bus handles," Gus brags as Dad revs the engine.

I find myself walking toward the bus with the sergeant, getting on right after he does, even though I have no idea why. I look back and see Gus climb into the passenger seat of the cruiser next to Dad. I watch the sergeant get settled in the driver's seat of the bus. Dad brings the cruiser up flush with the bus, like we're at the starting line to a NASCAR race.

I'm about to jump up and put an end to this craziness when Atticus leaps into the bus, takes the seat behind the driver across the aisle from me, and barks twice.

"Sounds like he just said 'Hit it,' " Laurence tells me.

"You got that right," a voice—mine?—calls out.

The cop revs the engine and peers through the windshield. Mia's standing about ten feet in front of us, between the cruiser and the bus, and she's raised her arm. I can't hear her, but I read her lips: *Three, two, one, go!* She drops her arm like she's waving a start flag.

Sergeant Laurence punches the gas pedal to the floor. For less than a second, the bus just roars, completely still as if held in place by a giant thumb, but then it leaps ahead with a sickening jolt that throws me back in my seat. The sergeant is screaming, Atticus is barking, I'm barely breathing, and we're smoking down the road.

I look out the window and see Dad in the lane next to us; he's grinning like the maniac he is and keeping the cruiser neck and neck with the bus. I take his picture from the window—a total blur.

And then it's over. We've passed the billboard—I don't even know who got there first. We tumble out of the bus and we're hooting and high-fiving and jumping around, punching the air and laughing uncontrollably.

"That, my friend, was a dead tie," Dad says to Sergeant Laurence. "But, man, these beasts kicked it into high gear."

"Sorry it's over." The cop wipes the sweat out of his eyes. "We should turn around and get back to your friends, though. We stranded those two on the side of the road."

"We could race backwards," Dad dares. I was right—he's all kinds of crazy. And, right now, the coolest guy on the planet. I must've caught speed fever, because it sounds like the best idea ever.

Laurence considers Dad's offer. I hope he doesn't point out that the cut in the road a few yards away would be perfect for turning the bus and the cruiser around to drive back. He squints down the highway. Dead calm. Not a car in sight.

"Tell you what: Let's split the difference. We'll drive

backwards—no sense driving any further trying to find a place to turn around"—he winks at me; he must have seen me staring at the turnaround—"but under the speed limit, and on the shoulder of the road, and make sure your hazard lights are on."

"That's a deal. See you on the flip side." Dad clambers back into the cruiser, waits for Gus to climb in, and then hurtles down the center of the highway in reverse. He's back to the starting point before I've taken two steps toward the bus.

"Yeah, I figured that's what he had in mind," Sergeant Laurence tells me as we climb back on board. I look at the driver's seat, then at him. I don't dare ask, but I'm hoping he'll read my mind.

"You're as nuts as your old man. Sorry, kid, you don't have a license. No driving." But he smiles. "I wish I could let you. But I've pushed this whole situation way too far. Anything more would be asking for trouble."

Once we're back by the cruiser, when I jump out of the bus to celebrate, the first thing I see is a new cop standing alongside *his* cruiser on the shoulder. He has his citation book out and a stunned look on his face.

Before I can make a sound, Sergeant Laurence leaps out of the bus, hooting and hollering, "Did you see us?"

The new cop clears his throat and takes a breath. I'm sure he's about to end the first cop's career and haul the rest of us to jail.

Sergeant Laurence looks at him, grins, and flips the bus keys to him. "Your turn, Captain Seavers. It. Is. Awesome. You can't believe you're driving a school bus. Feels more like a rocket or a torpedo."

Seavers looks like he doesn't know whether to holler or laugh. There's an agonizingly long pause while he studies the bus, then looks each of us up and down. Finally, he hands Dad the keys to the bus and turns to the first cop.

"Not today, son, but thanks for the offer. Of what, I'm not sure, since officially, I haven't been anywhere near this stretch of highway all day long. Marlene was worried when you radioed that you were taking a break, because you never take breaks, even when you're supposed to, and so I came out to make sure you were okay. Shame I couldn't find you. I must have been in the wrong place at the wrong time." He shrugs. "Catch you later, right?"

Captain Seavers tips his hat at Mia, slaps me on the back, and walks to his car. He pats the hood of the bus on his way.

Mia leans over and whispers to me: "See? What'd I tell you about the way guys bond over cars? Works every time."

We take a bunch of pictures of Dad and Gus leaning against the cop car and I look over to see Laurence and Mia entering each other's numbers on their phones.

Theo's going to be frosted about this if the cop is making a play for Mia.

When I get back on the bus, Theo's already in his seat, looking at a map. I hope he didn't miss the race. I try to remember when I lost sight of him after we got off the bus.

Before I can ask what he thought of the race or razz him about Mia and Sergeant Laurence, Dad yells, "Next stop: the shelter! Let's get that pup!"

We lurch off the shoulder and back onto the road. In the fast lane. Speeding, of course. Dad never learns.

As we drive off, I wave good-bye out the back window to the speck that is Sergeant Laurence.

ATTICUS

The race was the most fun I've had all day. We should have run, of course, and not driven, but my boss doesn't run. Can't blame him; only two legs.

I walk down the aisle and listen to everyone talk. Even the boss and my boy have more to say to each other. Talking is a good thing. Telling the truth is even better. I know when people lie, because their eyes get pinchy. Everyone on this bus has lied about something today. Lots of tight eyes and hunched-up shoulders. Lonely looks the same way; smells different, but looks just like lying.

They can fool each other, but not me.

Theo didn't like seeing the highway patrolman. He hid his face from the first one and he went to hide in the bus when the second cop showed up. He grabbed a map from the sunshade over the driver's seat and is tracing a line with his finger and nodding.

He's planning to run away.

The Big Picture

DONT B STOOPID.

That's the text Theo gets. I'm hanging over the back of his seat and can see his phone. He and Mia are sitting together. I'm right behind them. She's finally broken us down and we're playing rock-paper-scissors, which is the dumbest game ever, not to mention that the inside of my forearm is bright red and stinging from the finger slaps Theo whacks every time I lose. And I'm losing a lot. So when his phone buzzes, I'm glad for the distraction and in the perfect position to read his reply.

If his message were being sent in sign language, all he'd need to do is raise his middle finger.

"Uh, Theo? Everything cool?"

"Yeah. No. Everything's fine, I just don't want to play

anymore." He turns away to look out the window, ignoring Mia and me.

Theo's not just being rude, there's something weird about him. Mia glances at me and I know I'm not the only one who thinks that.

But she's not going to say anything and neither is Theo. I would, if I could think of the right words. I flop back in my seat and take a picture of my arm before the red marks fade.

I start scrolling through the pictures I've taken. Theo texting. Theo texting. Theo texting. Geez. Now I know why my mother goes berserk when she thinks I'm on my phone all the time. Super annoying.

I look at a picture I took of Atticus on the side of the road when we stopped for the race. Theo's in the background. I enlarge the image and I can tell he's trying to hide his face. From Sergeant Laurence? I squint harder at the screen. I wish I had a bigger screen and better resolution, because it's hard to tell for certain, but Theo looks like he's trying to be as invisible as he can. How did I miss that? Oh, yeah, I was focusing on Atticus.

What else didn't I see that I took a picture of? I flip through a few more shots to earlier in the day. I took a picture of the mess Theo made dumping his jacket and books and snacks out of his bag. When he first boarded the bus, he spread his stuff across his seat, to mark his territory, I guess. But now his area is neat and his duffel bag is packed.

Ready to go.

Go where?

Mia pokes Theo to get his attention. "Your energy is all messed up," she says, breaking the silence.

"You talk crazy sometimes."

He shrugs and tries to look out the window again. But Mia grabs him by the ear and pinches until he turns back to face her.

"Okay, how about this: I know something's going on with you, because you looked up and away when you said everything was fine."

"So?"

"That means you're lying. I can read energy fields *and* poker tells." Theo raises an eyebrow. "The diner had an after-hours card game. When I needed to pick up a few extra bucks, I'd sit in on a few games." Mia's got a lot of surprises up her sleeve.

"I don't know if she's right about you lying," I tell Theo, "but I've got about a million pictures of you texting and you look more and more worried all the time. What's going on?"

Theo fiddles with the piercing in his eyebrow. "I got in some trouble a while back and I gotta spend a couple months in the county jail."

"No way." I had no clue. He'd never mentioned this in all the time we studied together. How does a guy keep something like *this* to himself?

"Yeah, I talked to a couple guys I know who've been there and they said it's all right, like a really bad summer camp. I'm scheduled to turn myself in a couple of weeks from now."

"A couple of weeks?"

"Yeah. Because of overcrowding, they kind of stagger sentences in a low-security place like that."

"Overcrowding. Like the dog." Mia's voice is soft.

"I'm in good company," Theo tries to joke. But he doesn't pull it off. He sounds sick.

"There's more. What is it?" Mia's forcing him to look her in the eye.

"I screwed some people over to get a better deal. I gave up a few names and got some time taken off my sentence. They're not happy about it."

"Bobby?" Mia asks.

Theo nods. "He's one of 'em. I couldn't believe when we ran into him this morning. What're the odds of that? Forty miles from home and there he is."

"Bobby's the kind of guy who gets around." Mia makes a face like she tasted something bad.

"He's sending the texts?" I point to Theo's phone.

He frowns. "He's been following me. Us. Me. Whatever. Trying to freak me out so I change my mind, take back what I said. That was his car back there, the one that was on fire. He must have lost track of us when we made a pit stop, got ahead of the bus."

"And then burst into flames because he's pure evil," Mia adds.

"Yeah, but he wasn't anywhere near the car. So where is he? And is he alone? He probably called someone to come get him once his car crapped out. I really don't want to run into Bobby, especially not with any of his friends."

"So that's why your bag is packed?" I ask. "You were thinking of just slipping out of the bus?"

"Yeah. Thought it might be a better idea to take you guys out of the situation. I don't know what he's got planned if he catches up with me. Or if he's going to handle things himself or turn me in to the cops."

"Why would he turn you in?"

"I'm not actually supposed to leave home. Part of the deal was that I'd keep my nose clean and stick around the house until I had to turn myself in. I've been wondering . . . Bobby might think that would make the court think twice about the names I gave, maybe go easy on them or let them go. If it can be proved I wasn't sticking to the deal."

"So what if you got off the bus? You'd just disappear?"

"Yeah. I don't know if I can make things right. I'm

thinking about a fresh start somewhere new. Like maybe the trip and running into Bobby on the road were signs I was supposed to clear out."

"You should have told us what was going on," Mia says.

"Because you could help?" Theo frowns. I can't blame him; I'm skeptical.

"Yeah, matter of fact, I can. I knew someone needed to keep an eye on you if Bobby was in the picture."

"So you've been here to, what? Protect me?" Theo almost laughs.

"Something like that," Mia says.

"How's that work?"

"Bobby wasn't just going to walk away after trying to hit you."

"What, you read *his* aura and knew his plans?"

"No, I've played poker with Bobby and I know he's a cheating, thieving, lying snake who doesn't have a good bone in his miserable body. When I saw him take a swing at you and then walk away without a fight, I knew he had something more in mind."

"Oh."

"And you're not the only one who recognized Bobby's car back there. But I *was* the only one who talked to Sergeant Laurence about the fact we were probably being followed, and got his direct phone number."

"I wondered why you hitched a ride on a school bus with a bunch of strangers," I tell her.

"No, you didn't," Theo says. "You were just glad the hot chick got on the bus with us."

I turn red, but Mia doesn't seem to notice and keeps talking.

"I read your energy fields outside the diner. I knew you were good people and that I was supposed to help you. Your energy vibed with mine. Didn't you feel it?"

"Um . . . no," I say. And the only thing I feel now is scared. "What are we going to do about Bobby?"

"We could both run," Mia says, looking at Theo. "Just the two of us."

Huh. Isn't quitting your job and saving a dog enough for you? You want to run away and become a fugitive, too? And what about *me*? What's this "two" stuff?

"What's this 'we' stuff?" Theo asks her. "It's my problem."

"*You* might have gotten yourself in trouble," she tells him, "but *we're* getting you out. That's how trouble works. Don't ask me how I know."

I'm dying to ask how she knows. But instead, I say, "We've got to talk to my dad. He'll know what to do."

"No," Theo says. "I've already gotten you guys in way too deep. Next gas stop, I'm taking off. Bobby'll figure out I split, leave you alone, come looking for me."

"That's not how it's going to play out," Dad says.

Dad. He and Gus are sitting across the aisle, leaning forward. For how long? How did I *not* notice the bus had stopped and Dad and Gus were listening to us talk?

Dad warned me when I insisted on bringing Theo that something bad was going to happen. He also said he wouldn't lift a finger to help. I hope he's changed his mind. I hope he's got a good idea. And most of all, I hope he's been right all along and that things really will all work out. Theo could use that kind of thinking right now.

"Mia's right," Dad says. "This isn't something you're going to fix on your own. We'll figure something out. Together."

I start to feel better. Until I hear honking. Somebody is laying on their horn. I look out the window.

Bobby.

He's standing outside the bus next to a car, reaching through the open window to lean on the horn. Once he has our attention, Bobby gestures to Theo to get out of the bus.

Dad shakes his head. "No. You're not getting off." He takes a deep breath and starts to say more, but Mia waggles her phone at him and his face lights up. I don't know what code they're speaking that makes him change his mind, but he nods and says, "All right, let's do this. We're not sending Theo out there alone."

"Keep calm," Gus tells us. "Stick together. That guy's a bully, and bullies back down if ya stand up to 'em, show 'em you're not scared."

I'm the second one off the bus, after Theo and just before Dad. I look around the parking lot and shake my head. Just our luck today that Dad had to park in the creepiest, most deserted place on earth. There's not a soul around or another building that I can see. When did it get so dark? It's nighttime already; what time is it? Except for the bus's and the car's headlights, the parking lot is dark.

We're outside an abandoned haunted house. One of those roadside attractions. The shutters are hanging off the front windows, part of the roof has collapsed, and piles of garbage cover the front porch. There are fake—I hope—tombstones scattered around the front yard.

As Dad steps off the bus, I'm still looking around, trying to get my bearings and my night vision, when my whole world seems to explode because I'm shoved from the side, sent flying into Dad's arms. He keeps me from falling and then moves between me and Bobby, Gus on one side, Theo on the other, and Atticus in front of us. Theo grabs Mia's arm and pulls her behind him.

"That your little brother?" Bobby sneers at Theo.

"Yeah. He is. And he's got nothing to do with this."

"Says you. I say everyone here is a part of the trouble you got yourself in."

"Don't touch him again."

"Then be smart; come with me and we'll . . . figure out a way to fix things. Rethink the stories you told. Once you leave, I got no beef with anyone here."

Atticus growls and edges toward Bobby. Bobby glances down, remembers the attack on his ankle earlier in the day, and backs up a few feet. He notices Mia behind us.

"Mia? Nice. A little chubby, but—" It wasn't all that many hours ago that Mia knocked Bobby off his feet. He must have forgotten, talking that way. She reminds him when she steps in and knees him where the sun doesn't shine. He falls to his knees with a sickening, strangled half scream, half groan.

"I am not chubby." She glares down at him. "I told you not to talk to me like that. *And* you play a crappy hand of poker, you scum-sucking turd."

I hear a siren and a police car pulls into the parking lot. A Sergeant Laurence clone steps out of the car.

"One of you Joe Duffy?" he calls.

Dad nods, moves forward to shake his hand.

"I'm Lieutenant Spring, got a call from Sergeant Laurence a little while ago. He asked me to keep an eye on some of his friends as they were driving through our neck of the woods. He was worried they might run into some trouble, so we've been keeping an eye on you. A couple minutes ago, one of you texted him that there was need for assistance. Sergeant Laurence radioed me the info on Bobby. Turns out he's got a couple outstanding warrants and he stole that car. License plate was reported a couple hours ago. You did me a favor putting the drop on him like that."

That's why Mia waggled her phone at Dad and Dad let us all get out of the bus to confront Bobby. She'd been keeping in touch with Sergeant Laurence and Dad figured out what she meant.

Mia is one sharp girl. Dad's no dummy, either. I look over to smile at her and see that she and Theo are holding hands. I take a picture of them clutching each other. Then I snap Bobby on his knees, clutching his private parts and dry heaving a little. Atticus lifts his leg and pees, sprinkling Bobby. I take a picture of that, too. "Good boy."

"Bobby." Lieutenant Spring looks down at him. "On your feet, you know the drill."

"Thanks, Officer. Do you need to get statements from us?" Dad asks.

"Nah, Bobby's got a record long enough to keep us busy for a while. I understand you people are on the road to pick up a dog? I got one from the pound. I know what good friends they are. You take care of that dog. I'll handle Bobby."

The cop crams Bobby into the backseat and roars out of the parking lot. We climb back into the bus and slump in our seats, exhausted. This has been a busy day. I look around—a lot of gray faces.

Dad looks back at us in the rearview mirror.

"Everyone in favor of grabbing a few hours' sleep now that it's dark? Get a fresh start in the morning? We're not that far away now, and it's probably too late to get the dog today anyway. We'll get going first thing. I'll call the shelter tonight."

Four voices say yes and we drive off in search of a motel.

ATTICUS

I know better than to believe they've forgotten about that dog. No one's talking about it much, but we're getting closer. I can feel it. I'm glad we're going to stop and sleep in a bed. I can nap anywhere, but I like to do night in a bed. I usually sleep with my boy, but tonight I'm going to stay with Mia. I will growl if they try to make me change my mind. She's soft. I'm tired.

I raise my head to study my boy, Ben.

I'll be nice to this dog for Ben's sake. But I'll let the dog know there are rules and they will be followed. I know how to nip heels so it doesn't draw blood but can't be ignored.

I'm feeling better now that I know what to do.

Everyone always feels better when there's a plan.

9

The Bigger Picture

We check into a cheap but clean motel right off the highway. Dad's in the other bed in our room; Gus and Theo share a room on one side of us, and Mia and Atticus are on the other side. I'd whistled to Atticus to come with me, but he pretended not to hear and trotted into Mia's room. Theo rolled his eyes when he saw that.

Dad says we're only about an hour away from the puppy. If we pick him up first thing and the bus holds together and we don't have the kind of day we had today, we'll be sleeping in our own beds tomorrow night.

I'm so tired I think I'm not going to be able to keep my eyes open long enough to brush my teeth and drop into bed. But as soon as I'm lying there, I'm wide awake. Thinking.

I turn toward the other bed. "Dad? You awake?"

He flips on the light between our beds and grins at me. "Yeah. Tired as I am, I can't shut off my mind and fall asleep."

"Me too." He turns on the TV and starts channel surfing. I dig deep and make myself speak. "Dad? Why didn't you tell me about buying the house?"

He turns off the set and sits on the edge of his bed, his elbows on his thighs, looking at me.

"I know that sometimes my plans kind of freak you and your mother out."

"Always. And totally. But go on." He smiles at my lame attempt at a joke. I smile back.

"Mom and I have been talking about doing this for years. Even though we had a million reasons the business might not work out, we had to take the chance when the house came up for sale. But I was making her a nervous wreck with the cost of everything, and we didn't want to worry you. Especially not the last part of the school year, when you needed to keep your grades up."

"I see your point." I think for a minute. "I guess."

"Ben. I bought the house three months ago."

"You . . . But I thought . . . It sounded like . . . You didn't just buy it and quit your job on the same day?"

"Nope. I tried to tell you the whole story in the truck."

"Oh. I stopped listening because I was so mad."

"I've been working on the house all that time. I

90

thought if I could show you the business was already a success, you wouldn't be upset by the big change. And the risk."

"How far along is the house if you've been working that long?"

"Done!" Dad beams and pounds his knee. "Ten days ago, we got an offer. But it was iffy. We've been back and forth with offers and counteroffers. I've been going crazy waiting."

"You're not the most patient person."

"Exactly. And then the bill for hockey camp arrived. The timing couldn't have been worse. I wanted to be square with you, so I knew I had to tell you sooner than I'd planned. And to warn you that hockey camp wasn't a given. So when the email about the puppy came, it was the perfect excuse to do something other than sit around and worry."

"I'm glad you explained it. Can I tell you something?" He nods. "When I saw the haunted house today, I was worried you might get a craving for it. You know, because it had that possessed-by-demons-from-the-day-it-was-built look. And it seemed to be on top of a cemetery, which would probably make it great for ritual sacrifices. And that it might, I dunno, scream 'flip-worthy' to you."

"I actually called the realtor to see if the place was for sale. Good eye, son." He laughs at the expression on my face. "Gotcha! Imagine the work we'd have to do, huh, Ben? First the housing inspection, then the exorcism? Too much even for me."

We laugh and then I reach over and punch him on the shoulder, which, as everyone knows, is like a guy hug. Because he's Dad, I give him a big bear hug. Just like when I was little, we try to squeeze the breath out of each other. For the first time, he gives in first.

"What do you think is going to happen with the offer?" I ask.

"I think," he starts to say, and then, because I can read the look in his eye, we finish the sentence together, "it'll all work out."

Theo and Gus barge into our room like they own the place, Mia and Atticus on their heels.

"What's the matter with you people, not locking your door? Don't you know there are lunatics out there who'll rob you and kill you and hide your bodies under the mattress?" Gus says before he makes himself at home, propped up with pillows on my bed. He whistles to Atticus, who curls up at his side.

"We couldn't sleep," Theo explains.

"Too quiet and lonely," Mia agrees.

"Glad we're all together," Gus says. "I've been thinkin'. Got an announcement."

I look at Dad, Theo, and Mia and see I'm not the only curious one.

Gus wags his finger at Mia. "Yer crazy if ya think yer goin' back ta the kind of life where ya play cards with the likes of that Bobby character. I don't know where yer folks are or what ya think yer doin', but I'm steppin' in now. Ya need someone ta keep an eye on ya. I'm no kin ta ya, I know, but I don't hold truck with the crazy life ya got goin'. Okay with me if ya wanna talk silly energy field this or that, but ya gotta get a job where decent people spend their money, and you're gonna get an education. Do whatever you want after that. Read tarot cards at the county fair if ya wanna. Only yer gonna have some schoolin.'"

"Go on." I'd have thought Mia would put Gus in his place for talking to her like that, but she's intrigued. Me too.

"I've got a lady friend—" Gus pauses and blushes. "Runs a diner. She's always lookin' fer good help. Rents out an apartment over her garage. Good place; I did the wirin'. Once you've got a new job, new apartment, you can save fer school."

"I'd love that," Mia says. "Actually . . . I told you I had roommates, but I've been couch surfing the past couple of months. My roommate and I couldn't make rent and lost our apartment. I'd rather drink my own pee than move back home. And . . . maybe . . . You're right. I've been thinking about school. . . . I'm tired of auditions and rejections. The experience I'll get in college productions will help me when I turn professional later, right?"

We all nod even though no one knows if that's true. Atticus isn't the only one who wants to keep Mia around.

Then Gus turns to Theo, clears his throat, and bellows like a drill sergeant, "Minute we get back ta town, you an' me are gonna go see whoever it is ya need ta see about this time ya gotta do. Yer gonna get that hardware outta yer face"—he points to Theo's eyebrow piercing—"and pull up yer trousers, because no one wants ta see yer drawers. You'll do yer time like a man. Then yer gonna clean up yer act if I have ta kick yer keister every step of the way."

"Thanks, Gus, that's really nice of you." Theo's all red in the face, but he's smiling.

"I'm not nice." Gus harrumphs. "What's that silliness on your arm?" He points to Theo's wrist.

"It's a tattoo. Or a prototype. Figure I'll have it made permanent when I've done my time. A reminder."

"What is it?" Mia asks. We all lean forward and he shows us what he's drawn: a flying bus next to a grinning black and white dog.

Mia laughs. "Draw it on my ankle, maybe I'll have it made permanent, too." Theo turns red again when she puts her foot in his lap, and his hand shakes a little as he starts to draw.

"Then me," I say. "Go old-school, right on my bicep."

Theo draws tattoos on Mia and me while Gus and Dad look for something to watch on TV. They find an old movie about a guy trying to get somewhere and not doing a great job of it.

"By comparison, our trip has been relatively peaceful. It's all a matter of perspective," Dad explains to Gus. Atticus raises his head, looks at me, and yawns. He's as unimpressed by Dad's wisdom tonight as he was when I said almost that same thing to him earlier in the day.

"Yeah, right," Gus snorts. "When ya hafta compare yer day to that disaster ta find the upside, ya ain't in good shape."

I swear Atticus smiles at me before he lies back down. "It'll all work out," I tell Gus. "It always does."

Theo's done drawing tattoos on Mia and me, and I take pictures of them. Dad and Gus take a pass on his offer to ink them.

"Okay, now we've really got to get some sleep," Dad says, switching off the TV again. "We're wheels up at oh-five-hundred hours, so sleep fast."

We all say good night and everyone heads back to their rooms. Atticus stays on Dad's bed this time. As it should be.

"You might want to call Mom before you go to bed." I flip my phone to Dad. "Tell her we're okay. Tell her"—

I pause and then say it real fast before I can change my mind or something mean comes out of my mouth—"that I say hi, too, and I'm sorry I missed her calls and texts today."

Dad grins and tips his head in agreement as he dials her number and steps outside the room.

The perfect end to a perfectly weird day.

ATTICUS

Good thing that Gus is helping Theo and Mia. Someone's got to keep them straight, and they don't have me.

I heard him say that he raised everything on four legs on a farm.

Teenagers can't be that much different.

The Reason for the Trip

We pull up at the shelter where my new dog—I've settled on calling him Gretzky—has been staying. I leap out of the bus and race up the sidewalk.

The door is locked.

Dad, Gus, Mia, Theo, Atticus, and I are peering through the glass, and it's all I can do not to keep pressing the bell until someone answers. I think Theo's going to reach over me and start pounding with his fist. Mia's got her forehead pressed against the door, her hands cupped around her eyes, trying to see inside.

"Over here," a voice calls from the corner of the building.

We turn, and I see a cute girl gesturing at us to follow her to the back. She's holding a tiny gray kitten and a baby bottle. She looks like she's my age. And she's more than cute. I forget to breathe for a few seconds.

She leads us to a small fenced-in yard with a couple of kids' wading pools and a bunch of toys scattered around on the grass. She settles in a deck chair and starts feeding the kitten.

Atticus walks over and sniffs the kitten, nuzzling its tiny ears and licking one small paw. Then he sits next to the chair and watches the girl feed the cat. He nudges her hand when the bottle slips out of the kitten's mouth.

The girl is wearing a V L NT R apron and a badge that says AL S N. She's totally focused on feeding the cat and acts like we're not even standing there.

I find my voice, but it cracks. I clear my throat and try again. "We're here. Finally. It's been, well, it's a long story." I squint at her, trying to decipher the code on her apron.

"Volunteer. Alison. The shelter's on a tight budget, we can't afford vowels." She's funny. Joking, right? But she glares a hole in my forehead, then gives Dad, Theo, Gus, and Mia the once-over. She's petting Atticus's head with her free hand without seeming to notice. He rests his head on her knee, studying the kitten. "You're the people for Conor?"

Weird. People who like animals, in my experience, are usually friendly. Maybe she doesn't like people.

"Who's Conor?"

"The border collie. His name is Conor. I might not be able to keep him, but at least I can give him the most beautiful name I know."

"Oh, we didn't know he had a name. I was going to call him . . . Never mind," I stumble. "We didn't know you wanted to keep him." Man, I didn't see *this* coming. "But, yeah, we're here. For . . . Conor."

"No."

"What do you mean, 'no'?" Now that we finally got here, we're . . . denied? Can she do that? *Why* would she do that?

"What makes you think you're good enough for Conor?" She's unfazed that this homeless dog has a welcoming committee of five and another border collie and that we arrived on a school bus. What does it take to make a good impression on this girl?

"Good enough?" Uh, we're *here*. And we *want* him. What else are you looking for? I bite my tongue because a snotty response isn't going to help.

"Mr. Duffy and Ben came all this way—and so did the rest of us—just to give the dog a home," Theo pitches in. "You can trust them. Ben'll take good care of him, of Conor; they're excellent dog owners."

"It's a dog, for crying out loud," Gus says. "You're not handing out honorary titles here." He snorts and shakes his head. For once, Gus's annoyance is on point. I wish he'd take it up a notch and bully her into giving us the dog.

"Uh, sweetie?" Mia says. "Is your boss around? Can we talk to a grown-up?"

Alison finally looks up from the baby cat. "I've known Conor since he's been at the shelter. He's special. There's something about border collies that make you feel like they're looking at you and reading your soul."

"You're not telling us anything we don't already know," I say.

"Then you know I can't go handing out border collies to just anyone."

"It's hard to argue when you put it like that, but—"

"Besides, there's already someone here to get him. Inside."

No.

Oh, no.

I see the picture of the puppy on Dad's phone in my mind and it hits me how much I want this dog. I haven't been thinking about him much, I know. First I was so mad at Dad and then I got caught up with all the new people and the trip and Conor kind of slipped my mind.

But now that we won't be taking him home, my heart aches. I think back to how awful I felt when Dad told me I might not go to hockey camp; at that moment, I thought it was the worst feeling I'd ever know. But it's nothing compared to hearing I'm not going to get Conor.

"Well, can't you talk to the other person and explain that there's been a mix-up and that the dog is ours, was promised to us, and we drove a long way, a *loooooooong* way to get him and—"

"That won't be necessary." I'm cut off midsentence.

BY MOM.

Who's standing right behind me with a wiggling border collie puppy on a leash.

Mom is here.

There are a few blurry minutes where Mom and I are hugging and I'm on my knees hugging Conor and then Mom is being introduced to and hugging Gus and Theo and Mia. Then Mom and Dad hug while the rest of us hug Alison and the kitten she's still cradling and laugh that she and Mom pulled it off and gave us such a hard time. I take a picture of Mia and Theo hugging—he seems to hold on an extra long time, but I can't blame him since I did the same thing with Alison. There's a lot of hugging.

Until Atticus barks.

We all turn and look at him. He's watching Conor.

Conor whines back at him.

Atticus pads over to Conor and they start wagging their tails and circling each other, doing that butt- and ear-smelling thing. Once acquainted, they sit facing each other like mirror images, taking stock.

They belong together.

I look up from the dogs and see Mom and Dad watching them, too. He's got his arm around her and she's leaning her head against his shoulder.

"So, uh, what's up?" I ask.

"I couldn't resist pulling your leg like that, so I jumped in the car. Made way better time than you all did. You two are always going off doing things together. I feel a little left out sometimes. This seemed like a dramatic way to make an entrance. Like something Dad would do."

"Good one."

"Besides, I have excellent news: The house sold—we have a deal."

"We?"

"The company is called Duffy and Son. The 'and Mom, too' is implied." She smiles.

"Dad flipped his first house." I'm proud of him. He *did* know what he was doing.

"*We* flipped *our* first house," Dad says.

"And we put an offer in on a second one," Mom tells me. Even Dad looks surprised. "Strike while the iron's hot, right?"

"That's a very Dad-like move, Mom."

"It wouldn't hurt if we all tried something new from time to time," she says, smiling.

"Because it'll all work out," Dad and I say together.

"I'm taking this one." Gus is walking out of the shelter with a teacup Chihuahua tucked in the bib of his overalls. The dog's tiny head and front paws pop out the top, like he's in one of those baby-carrier things. "Sign on his cage says his name is Gizmo. A garage can't have too many gizmos."

I take their picture. Alison's looking at me and Theo. "Are you brothers?"

"Yes," Theo and I answer together.

"We all belong to each other," Mia adds.

"Family," Gus says.

"And I need to get a picture," I say. "Everyone huddle up with the dogs." I hand my phone to Alison to take a group shot and jump in the middle.

She's scrolling through my photos by the time I get back to her side to get my phone back. "These are really good," she tells me. "You should take pictures of the dogs we're trying to find homes for to post online. The better the picture, the better chance the dog has of finding a home. C'mon, I'll show you the rest of them." She takes my arm. I let her.

I look back as I walk inside. Dad and Mom are leaning against the fence, his arm around her shoulder, watching Atticus and Conor play in the yard. Theo and Mia are each feeding a kitten they scooped up from a box in the shade. And Gus is making kissy faces at Gizmo.

Alison and I take pictures of all the animals and exchange phone numbers and email addresses and we Facebook friend each other on my phone. Then we head back to the crowd in the yard.

Alison sinks to her knees and buries her face in Conor's ruff to wipe her ears in his fur and to kiss him good-bye. "I love you. Everything in me knows that they're good enough for you." She reaches down and unties her vowel-less apron, pulling it off and handing it to me. "Will you take this for him? It's got my smell. Maybe that way he won't forget me."

I take the apron and she hugs me. Mia feeds Conor a few potato chips from the bag she's saved from the last rest stop, and Gus pets his silky ears. Theo puts his hand in front of the puppy and says, "High five, little dude," and then laughs when Conor licks his fingers. Dad drops to one knee and watches the puppy chew on his shoelace. Conor likes everyone; he greets them with kisses and wiggles. But he always looks back to Atticus and Mom. Them, he loves.

"Will you come to the shelter's fund-raiser this fall?" Alison asks. "We're going to have food and games and a silent auction, and people who have adopted animals will come back and tell how they found each other. I think you'll have the best story."

"We've got our own bus, so transportation isn't an issue." I point to the bus at the curb. "In fact, we might still be on our way back home by the time the party happens."

"You never know." Her smile. Whoa.

Everything *does* work out.

ATTICUS

I wish the boss and my boy had told me they were getting someone like me. I wouldn't have worried. I thought we were just getting a dog.

At Alison's shelter, there were eight dogs Conor and I had to keep in line. We scared them with our piercing gaze. Everyone was afraid of our dropped shoulders and raised rumps—it was like we hypnotized them. A couple of the younger dogs who didn't get what was happening tried wandering away, but we straightened them out real fast.

We work together like we were born for it.

We were happy to get back to the bus and get everyone on. See our new family heading back home.

We got in the car with the real boss, the one who smells like flowers. Enough with the bus. The car doesn't bounce and the real boss doesn't sing or speed. I was ready for a nap. Conor and I curled up in the backseat and slept all the way home.

This is going to work out just fine, we agree.

11

The Time After

Today's the last day of summer. Feels like it was just a minute ago that vacation and the road trip started.

In hindsight, I can see that Dad's plan turned out fine, just like he always says it will. I can hardly remember why I didn't want to go or being mad at my parents or upset about hockey camp.

When we left the shelter, Mom had to get back home to work, so she took Conor and Atticus in the car with her.

No one on the bus was in a real hurry to get back, not even me. So it was easy for Dad and Mia to talk us into doing touristy things that we hadn't had time for on the way to get Conor. Theo and Gus and I pretended to grumble, but we had the best time of all, I think.

We saw scale replicas of the great architectural works

of Frank Lloyd Wright constructed out of sugar cubes. We stopped at souvenir shops and ate pecan logs until we were sick from the sugar, and bought dribble mugs and trucker hats and T-shirts, and had our pictures taken poking our heads through holes in painted plywood that made us look like bullfighters and mermaids and cowboys and giant spiders.

We went to an amusement park and broke the record riding the roller coaster the most times. Theo and I were barfy for most of the day, and Dad and Gus had to divvy up driving because of their dizziness, but it was worth it to get the certificate and have our picture taken for the wall of fame.

We won a few bucks at the racetrack, too, enough to pay for gas, motels, and food. We needed a couple races to get the hang of betting, and we all had different techniques for choosing the right horse and jockey. Everyone bet on Conor's Friend. We couldn't resist. He didn't win, but that didn't stop us from running to the paddock to have our picture taken with him. The jockey said he'd never ridden such a popular fourth-place mount before.

We hit a state fair, too, and won a karaoke contest. We sang "On the Road Again," natch, and no one could touch us. Dad took credit for the win because he claimed we'd all been inspired by the country music stations he plays.

We finally rolled back home after a few days, sun-burned and carsick. But we'd been checking in with Mom every day. I called her a lot and Dad talked to her every night. I'd see him wandering around the parking lot of each motel with his phone. Talking and listening. And laughing.

Things aren't perfect at home; Mom still spends way too much time at the kitchen table surrounded by the checkbook and a stack of bills, and Dad works crazy sick hours on the houses. But we eat dinner together every night and Dad's moved back into their room. That's a start.

As soon as the first house sold, Dad closed on the second house. Before that project was complete, he bought a third place. He hired a couple guys part-time to help him out, and he taught me to hang drywall. We're taking a drive after dinner to look at another property. See if it has potential.

Turned out we had money in time to get me to hockey camp after all. But I didn't want to go. Not when Duffy and Son had so much work lined up. I'll go next summer. I'll go every summer if we keep working this hard. I joined a summer league at a rink in town so I didn't have to miss hockey altogether. Worked out for the best; those older guys really pushed me and I've got mad skills now. Probably as good as what I'd've picked up at camp. Made a bunch of new friends, too.

I'm not sure what's going to happen with our business, because you just never know, but if I've learned one thing this summer, it's that great things can happen from little starts.

Oh, and that everything works out.

Conor and Atticus figured out how to live together, just like Dad said they would. Probably because neither of them thinks they're a dog. Conor and I get along fine, but he's decided he belongs to Mom, not me, after all. Dad promised that the very next border collie rescue he hears about, that'll be my dog.

I can't wait. Because another thing I learned this summer is that good things come in sets of three: Theo, Gus, and Mia, the three houses, and, pretty soon, three border collies.

Gus comes over every weekend. To bring Gizmo to see Conor and Atticus and to make sure Dad doesn't violate building code with the wiring in his houses. Gizmo hasn't touched the ground except to pee since Gus picked him up at Alison's shelter and shoved him in the front of his bib.

Mia and Theo aren't a couple, even though that's what he'd like. They're Just Friends, she always says. He winks at me and shakes his head behind her back, hopeful. He's going to have to get past Atticus first. Atticus thinks no one sees that he won't let Theo sit by Mia even now that we're off the bus. But I notice.

Mia works at Gus's lady friend's diner and lives above her garage, just like Gus promised. It's a good job—no creepy customers—and she's saving for school.

Theo wound up only having to do about two weeks at the county lockup because of overcrowding and his good behavior. We had a huge pizza party for him when he was released. He's working at Gus's garage, and after fall semester, he'll have enough credits to graduate from high school. He's trying to talk Mia into enrolling at the same community college so they can be roommates. She shakes her head about living together, but she doesn't say no to going to the same school, and the last time they were over, they were looking through a course catalog with Gus.

I finally posted a bunch of pictures from the road trip on my Facebook page. There are shots of tattoos, bloody Kleenex, cops and paramedics and firemen jumping off their rigs, two border collies and a teacup Chihuahua and close-up portraits of eight other rescue dogs, a roller coaster record certificate, a racehorse and his jockey, and the talent-show stage at the state fair.

If you don't know the whole story, the page looks like a lot of crazy. The pictures crack me up.

No one turned out to be like I thought they would. I wonder if they think the same about me. I know I sure do.

Lastly, I look at a picture of Alison. Like Theo and

Mia, we're Just Friends. Like Theo, I like her more than that, even with the long distance. We keep in touch, and I'm hoping.

Next month, we're all going to the shelter's fund-raiser. All back on the bus, with Atticus and Conor. We couldn't go anywhere without them. Not that they'd let us—now Dad and I have two border collies trying to get in the truck every time we go anywhere. They work as a team and run the whole house.

Plus, Conor's the poster boy for the shelter. I sent Alison a picture I took of him and she talked the committee into using it on the website.

He should play a big role.

He brought us all together.

About the Authors

Gary Paulsen is the distinguished author of many critically acclaimed books for young people, including three Newbery Honor Books: *The Winter Room, Hatchet,* and *Dogsong.* He won the Margaret A. Edwards Award given by the ALA for his lifetime achievement in young adult literature. Among his Random House books are *Crush; Paintings from the Cave; Flat Broke; Liar, Liar; Woods Runner; Masters of Disaster; Lawn Boy; Lawn Boy Returns; Notes from the Dog; Mudshark; The Legend of Bass Reeves; How Angel Peterson Got His Name; Guts: The True Stories Behind* Hatchet *and the Brian Books; The Beet Fields; Soldier's Heart; Brian's Return, Brian's Winter,* and *Brian's Hunt* (companions to *Hatchet*); and five books about Francis Tucket's adventures in the Old West. Gary Paulsen has also published fiction and nonfiction for adults. His wife, Ruth Wright Paulsen, is an artist who has illustrated several of his books. He divides his time between his home in Alaska, his ranch in New Mexico, and his sailboat on the Pacific Ocean. You can visit him on the Web at GaryPaulsen.com.

Jim Paulsen is a sculptor and former elementary school teacher. He lives with his wife and two children in Minnesota. *Road Trip* is his first book.

Gary Paulsen is available for select readings and lectures. To inquire about a possible appearance, please contact the Random House Speakers Bureau at rhspeakers@random house.com.